1st half a *the war*

SNEAK THIEVES

Billy Swan was riding Nighthawk when he heard the faint sound of hooves on rock. Since the herd was at rest, he looked around to find the source of the sound and saw a long dark line ragged with heads and horns moving away from the main herd.

"Cattle thieves!" he shouted.

Billy's shout not only awakened his partners—it alerted the thieves and instantly one of them fired a shot. Billy fired back. By now, a barrage began coming from the camp itself as James and the others rolled out of their blankets and began shooting. Revelation was standing in the wagon, firing a rifle.

Billy put his pistol away and raised his rifle. He aimed toward the dust and the swirling melee of cattle, waiting for one of the robbers to present a target. One horse appeared, but its saddle was empty.

Then another horse appeared, this time with a rider who was shooting wildly. . . .

Ralph Compton

The Bozeman Trail

———

A Ralph Compton Novel
by Robert Vaughan

A SIGNET BOOK

SIGNET
Published by New American Library, a division of
Penguin Putnam Inc., 375 Hudson Street,
New York, New York 10014, U.S.A.
Penguin Books Ltd, 80 Strand,
London WC2R 0RL, England
Penguin Books Australia Ltd, Ringwood,
Victoria, Australia
Penguin Books Canada Ltd, 10 Alcorn Avenue,
Toronto, Ontario, Canada M4V 3B2
Penguin Books (N.Z.) Ltd, 182–190 Wairau Road,
Auckland 10, New Zealand

Penguin Books Ltd, Registered Offices:
Harmondsworth, Middlesex, England

First published by Signet, an imprint of New American Library,
a division of Penguin Putnam Inc.

First Printing, September 2002
10 9 8 7 6 5 4 3 2 1

Printed in the United States of America

PUBLISHER'S NOTE
This is a work of fiction. Names, characters, places, and incidents either
are the product of the author's imagination or are used fictitiously,
and any resemblance to actual persons, living or dead, events, or locales
is entirely coincidental.

BOOKS ARE AVAILABLE AT QUANTITY DISCOUNTS WHEN USED TO PROMOTE
PRODUCTS OR SERVICES. FOR INFORMATION PLEASE WRITE TO PREMIUM
MARKETING DIVISION, PENGUIN PUTNAM INC., 375 HUDSON STREET, NEW YORK,
NEW YORK 10014.

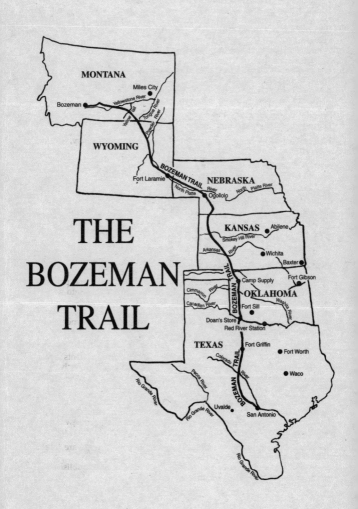

THE
BOZEMAN
TRAIL

MONTANA

Miles City

Bozeman

Yellowstone River

Yellow Trail

Tongue River

Powder River

WYOMING

BOZEMAN TRAIL

Fort Laramie

NEBRASKA

North Platte River

Ogollolo

North Platte River

KANSAS

Abilene

Smokey Hill River

Arkansas River

Wichita

Baxter

Camp Supply

Fort Gibson

Cimmarron River

BOZEMAN TRAIL

OKLAHOMA

Canadian River

Washita River

Fort Sill

Doan's Store

Red River Station

TEXAS

Fort Griffin

Fort Worth

Colorado River

Waco

Rio Grande River

Pecos River

Colorado River

BOZEMAN TRAIL

Uvalde

Rio Grande River

San Antonio

Rio Grande River

Chapter One

Atacosa Creek, Bexar County, Texas
Thursday, June 20, 1861:

James Cason was bent low over his mount's neck. The horse's mane and tail were streaming out behind, its nostrils flaring wide as it worked the powerful muscles in its shoulders and haunches. Bob Ferguson was riding just behind James, urging his animal to keep pace, and Billy Swan was riding beside him. Behind James, Bob, and Billy, rode three more cowboys from Long Shadow Ranch.

The six men hit the shallow Atacosa Creek in full stride, and sand and silver bubbles flew up in a sheet of spray, sustained by the churning action of the horses' hooves until huge drops began falling back like rain. James led the men toward an island in the middle of the stream.

"We'll hold here!" James shouted.

The six riders brought their steeds to a halt.

In one case the halting action was so abrupt that the horse almost slipped down onto its haunches in response to the desperate demand of its rider.

The six men had been in pursuit of a group of Mexican banditos who had murdered two of Long Shadow's cowboys and stolen a hundred head of cattle. Long Shadow was a ranch of over one hundred thousand acres, located just south of San Antonio de Bexar. The ranch was owned by Colonel Garrison Cason, James Cason's father.

Unbeknownst to the boys, the small band of raiders they were pursuing was but a part of a group of nearly one hundred Mexican outlaws who crossed the border into America to conduct raids on ranches all over South Texas. This outlaw army, led by a former guerrilla who called himself "General" Ramos Garza, planned to steal a large herd, then retreat across the border back into Mexico where they would be safe from any further pursuit.

Thinking only they were pursuing a few murderous rustlers, the boys had ridden right into Garza's army. When that happened, the pursuers became the pursued, and the small posse was forced into a desperate dash back to a small island in the middle of the stream.

"How many are there?" James asked. "Did anyone get a count?"

"Too many to fight off!" Billy answered.

2

Of the six, Billy Swan was the only one who was not from Long Shadow. Billy lived with his uncle on Trailback, a neighboring ranch. But a rustler who stole from one rancher stole from them all, so cooperation among the ranchers against rustlers was routine.

Billy would have ridden with them at any rate, first because he was a friend, and secondly because it was an adventure and Billy never turned his back on any adventure. As it was developing, however, this was a little more adventure than even he had planned on.

"We'd better get ready," James said. "We'll be making our stand here."

James Cason was twenty-two years old. He was a rangy, raw-boned man with a handlebar mustache and eyes and demeanor that were older than his years.

"James, we can't stay here! We got to skedaddle!" Carl, one of the cowboys, said.

"Skedaddle to where?" James asked. "We were running as hard as we could, just to get here."

"Maybe if we surrender," Carl suggested.

"Surrender and do what? Get our skin peeled?" Bob Ferguson asked. "That bunch out there is part Mexican, part Comanche, and part rattlesnake. They eat live scorpions for fun. You want to surrender to them?"

Bob was a year younger and, at five-foot-eight, six inches shorter than James. He was an exceptionally skilled rider who often earned money by riding, and winning, impromptu races. Bob's father, Dusty, had been Garrison Cason's ranch foreman for nearly twenty years. As a result, Bob, too, grew up on Long Shadow, and he and James had been friends for as long as either could remember.

"No," Carl said. "I don't think I would want that."

"Me, neither," Bob said.

James pointed to the neck of the island, which faced the eastern bank of the creek, the direction from which they had just come.

"I think our best bet is to try and squirm down through the tall grass. We'll take positions as near to the point as we can get, and do as much damage as we can when they start across the water."

"You think we can stop them?" one of the other cowboys asked.

"We'll know the answer to that in about two minutes," James said. "Now hurry, get into position. And try and stay out of sight. Carl, you take that tree, Joe, that stump, Syl, you go over there behind that rock. Billy, this fallen tree is large enough for both of us, you stay here with me."

As the cowboys rushed to take up their positions, James shouted more instructions. "Don't be spooked into shooting when you hear them. I want you to hold your fire until I give the word. Hold it until the last possible moment. Then make your shots count!"

"James, you didn't say where you wanted me," Bob said.

"I want you to go for help."

"What?"

"You are the best rider here. I want you to get back to the ranch. Tell my father where we are. Tell him to bring help as fast as he can. We'll hold them off for as long as possible. If he gets here soon enough, some of us may still be alive."

"No, James, don't make me do this!" Bob protested. "I don't aim to show my tail while the rest of you are stayin' here to face them."

"Oh for God's sake, Bob, do it!" Billy said. "Do you think any of us would actually think you are running?"

"Don't you understand, Bob? If you don't go for help, none of us are going to get out of this alive!" James said.

Bob looked at the others.

"Do it, Bob," Carl Adams said. He was the youngest of the group. "You are our only chance."

"Yes, do it! Go!" Joe and Syl shouted.

"All right," Bob said. "Billy, if you don't mind, I'd like to take Diablo," Bob said. "He's the fastest horse."

"He's yours," Billy replied. "Just get through!"

Billy brought Diablo up, and quickly, Bob put his foot into the stirrup, then swung up into the saddle.

"Good luck!" Billy shouted, slapping Diablo on the rump. The others shouted as well, as Bob hit the water on the west side of the Atacosa, away from where the main body of their pursuers were. James watched Bob gallop north along the west bank of the creek until Diablo crested an embankment, then he turned back to await the banditos.

"I hear them!" Joe said. His announcement wasn't necessary, however, for by then everyone could hear the drumming of the hoofbeats as well as the cries of the banditos themselves, yipping and barking and screaming at the top of their lungs.

The banditos crested the bluff just before the creek; then, without a pause, they rushed down the hill toward the water, their horses sounding like thunder.

"Remember, boys, hold your fire!" James shouted. "Hold your fire until I give you the word!"

The banditos stopped just at the water's edge, then holding their rifles over their heads, began

6

shouting guttural challenges to the men who were dug in on the island.

"Gringos! Are you ready to die, gringos?"

"I think maybe we will kill all of you!"

"Get ready," James called.

The banditos rushed into the water, riding hard across the fifty-yard-wide shallows, shouting and gesturing with rifles and pistols. Then three of them pulled ahead of the others, and when they were halfway across the water, James gave the order to fire. All three of the outlaws went down.

James had fired in concert with the others, and saw the bandito he shot go down as if he had been knocked from his saddle with a club.

The cowboys' devastating volley was effective, for the banditos who survived swerved to the right and left, riding by, rather than over the cowboys' positions.

The remaining banditos crossed the creek, then started up the sandy point on the opposite side. They regrouped on the west bank; then turned and rode back for another charge. They were met with a second volley, as crushing as the first had been. Again, a significant number of the banditos in the middle of the charge went down.

The Mexicans pulled back to the east bank of the stream to regroup, watched anxiously by the cowboys on the island. By now the stream was strewn with dead and dying banditos. There were at least eight or nine of them, lying face-down in the shallow water as the current parted around them.

"Has anyone been hit?" James called.

All five men with James answered in the negative. So far, no one had been scratched.

"How are you doing on bullets?" James asked. "Do you all have enough?"

"I'm running out of ammunition," Syl said.

James took off his belt and started pushing cartridges out of the little leather loops. "Let's divide up what we have left," he suggested.

"Looks like they're about to come at us again," Billy said.

"All right, boys, get ready. They're comin' back," James shouted.

James got down behind the log and rested the barrel of his rifle on the top. The advantage of the rifle was its range and accuracy. The disadvantage was the time it would take to reload.

He would fire the rifle first, then if they continued to press their attack, he would use his pistol. Although the pistol held six charges, it was only accurate at close range.

He thumbed back the hammer of his rifle, sighted down the long barrel, and waited.

The banditos came again, their horses leaping over the bodies of their comrades and horses. One of the banditos wore a bright red serape and a sombrero decorated with silver. He was riding at the head of the others, and James was sure he must be the leader. That was the one James selected as his target. He waited for a good shot.

When the shot presented itself, James squeezed the trigger. His bullet hit the Mexican just above the right ear, then exited through the top of his head. James saw brain tissue, blood, and bone detritus erupt from the top of the man's head. The bandito dropped his pistol as he pitched back off his horse.

When they saw their leader go down, the others milled about for a moment, uncertain as to what they should do. One or two started forward, but it wasn't a concerted charge and, like their leader, they were easily shot down.

By now, nearly a dozen Mexicans lay dead on the banks of the Atacosa, in the water, and on the sandy beaches of the island. The Mexicans made one more charge, and during this charge, James felt a blow to his left thigh. There was very little pain and he thought, perhaps, a rock had been kicked up by one of the horses' hooves.

Once again the Mexicans were repulsed and, once again, not one of James's men had been lost. But their defense of the island had not been without some cost, for James had been wounded. What he had thought to be a blow

9

from a rock turned out to be a bullet wound, and as he looked down toward his thigh he could see that the front of his pants was wet and sticky with blood. Fortunately, it didn't seem to be gushing, which meant that no artery had been struck.

The banditos did not make another attempt against the island. Instead, they crossed over the river in considerable numbers, both upstream and down, so they could occupy positions in the surrounding bluffs on both sides of the stream. In this way they were able to keep the cowboys effectively trapped on the island.

"What are they doing?" Carl asked, nervously. "Why don't they come on?"

"They are going to wait us out," Billy said.

"Come on, you cowards!" the young cowboy shouted. "Come and get us!"

"Take it easy, Carl. You're doing just what they want you to do," James said.

From across the water, they heard laughter.

"Do not be in such a hurry to die, amigo. We will kill you soon enough, I think."

The taunt was followed by more laughter.

James knew that their survival depended upon whether or not Bob was able to get through to his father. If Bob made it, James's father would no doubt be able to effect a rescue by nightfall. But if Bob didn't make it, if he had been caught and killed by the banditos, it would only be a matter of time until the taunting Mexican made good his threat.

There was sporadic firing throughout the rest of the afternoon and early evening as the cowboys on the island and the banditos on the bluffs continued to exchange gunfire. After sunset that evening, James counted half a dozen campfires scattered about on both sides of the creek. He and the others on the island listened as the banditos laughed and shouted insults and challenges to the little group on the island.

"Who the hell are these guys?" James asked. "It looks like a whole army of them."

"It is an army," Billy said.

"What do you mean?" Joe asked.

"They call themselves guerrillas," Billy explained. "You see, right now the French control Mexico, but they don't control the peasants. Every now and then, someone will get a bunch of men together, call himself a general, and tell them they are a revolutionary army, fighting for their freedom."

"Well, what the hell are they fightin' us for?" Carl asked. "We ain't took away their freedom."

"No, we haven't. But anything, even the outlaw trail, is better than what they have."

Billy Swan knew what he was talking about. He had been born to a Mexican mother in the border town of El Paso. Four years ago he had come to San Antonio de Bexar to live with his father's brother, Loomis Swan. Billy and James had been good friends ever since.

With his dark complexion and flashing black eyes, Billy could easily pass as Mexican. He was fluent in Spanish and was as likely to be found in the Mexican cantinas as he was in the American saloons. He was good with ropes, and could drop a loop over a steer while riding at top speed. He was also skilled with a knife, and it was said that the reason he had come to live with his uncle was because he had killed a man in El Paso. But Billy had never confirmed the rumor, and James had never asked him about it.

As James and the others looked anxiously out into the night, they discussed among themselves whether or not Bob made it.

"Sure, he got through. He was on the fastest horse in the county," Joe said.

"And he's the best rider," Carl insisted.

"Yes, but he had a long way to go, and Diablo was tired," Syl said, adding a precautionary note to the discussion.

"Don't be worrying about Bob Ferguson," Billy said reassuringly. "He is the best horseman I've ever known. He can get more out of a burro than most men can from a quarter horse."

James listened to the conversation of the others, but it was becoming increasingly difficult to pay attention. The initial shock of his wound had long since worn off, and now waves of pain were washing over him. The bullet was going to have to come out.

It wasn't something he was looking forward to, but he knew he couldn't put it off any longer.

He limped over to Billy.

"How are you doing?" Billy asked.

"I want you to cut this bullet out of my thigh," he said.

Billy looked at the ugly, jagged wound. "I don't know, James, I'm not very good at that sort of thing," he said. "That wound is awfully close to a main artery. If the knife slipped and I cut it—you could bleed to death."

"I'd rather bleed to death than die of gangrene," James said. "Which is exactly what I'm going to do if I don't get that bullet out. Besides, I've always heard you were good with a knife. Now's my chance to find out."

Billy sighed. "All right, I'll take the bullet out for you." He looked around at the others. "Carl, there's a bottle of tequila in the saddlebag of Bob's horse. Bring it to me."

"Bob was carrying tequila?"

"No, I was. I switched it when I gave Bob my horse."

Carl brought the bottle back to Billy. By the time he returned, Billy had cut open James's pants so he could get to the wound. With his teeth, he pulled the cork from the bottle and poured tequila over the wound. It stung, but the effect was to wash away the blood and expose the ugly black hole where the bullet had entered the flesh. After that, he poured tequila over the knife. He looked at James and smiled.

"It's a good thing I like you," he said. "I wouldn't waste good tequila like this on just anyone."

James managed a pained laugh.

"Are you ready?" Billy asked.

"Wait," James said. He picked up a stick, put it in his mouth, then nodded.

"A couple of you boys hold open the wound," Billy said, showing what he wanted them to do.

The two men put their hands on each side of the wound then began stretching it open. One of the others held a burning brand aloft so Billy could see what he was doing and, carefully, he dug into the flesh until he located the bullet. Then, using the blade as a wedge, he got beneath the spent missile and pried it out.

"Uhn," James grunted as he spit out the stick. "That wasn't all that bad."

"It isn't over. We're going to have to cauterize it," Billy said.

"Yeah, I know," James said. He picked the stick up again. "All right, let's do it."

Billy tore open a couple of the paper cartridges, and poured a little pile of gunpowder over the wound, then ignited it. It made a big flash and James cried out, then he bit the cry off. There was the smell of burned powder and seared flesh.

"Are you all right?" Billy asked.

"Yeah," James replied in a strained voice. "Thanks, Billy."

Billy nodded, then walked over to sit under a tree. Taking out his pipe he filled it with tobacco, then lit it up and was puffing contentedly when James came over to join him.

"Are you going to make it?" Billy asked.

"It hurts like hell," James said. "But I'll be able to hold up my end when they come back. If they come back," he added.

"What do you mean, if they come back?"

"I'm not sure, but what I may have killed their leader." He described the man he shot. "You say he was wearing a red serape?" he asked.

"Yes. You didn't see him?"

"No," Billy answered. "But there's a fella named Garza, Ramos Garza, who is one of those revolutionary generals I was telling you about. He wears a red serape."

"You think this was him?"

"It could just be someone else copying him," Billy said. "Although with a group this large, I'd say the chances might be pretty good that it was Garza you shot."

"Will that stop them?"

"I don't know," Billy said. "But it will sure

slow them down until they decide who their new leader is going to be."

"Maybe that's all we need," James said. "Just a little more time until Bob gets back."

Billy was silent for a moment before he replied. "Have you considered the possibility that Bob might not come back?" he asked. "Maybe something happened to him. Seems to me like he's had plenty of time to ride to the ranch and back by now."

"I know. I've thought about it and I would be lying to you if I said I wasn't a little worried. But I'm not ready to give up on him yet."

"Still, you'd think he'd be—"

"James, Billy, they're comin' back again!" Carl called.

"We'd better get ready," James said, straining to get to his feet.

As they were getting into position, they heard shots being fired, but the shots weren't being fired at them.

"It's Pa!" James said, happily. "Bob got through! I told you he would!"

Flashes lit up the night as gunfire erupted between the banditos still encamped around the island and the large group of Texas ranchers who had ridden in with Garrison Cason. The fight was furious and brief as the little bandito army scattered, leaving their rustled herd behind them.

The Texans rode across the Atacosa at a full gallop.

"James!" Garrison called. "James, where are you?"

"Here, Pa," James said, standing up from his place of cover. Riding alongside Garrison Cason was Bob Ferguson and Bob's father, Dusty. Billy's uncle, Loomis Swan, was also part of the posse, as were several other ranchers and cowboys. Cason had put together an army of his own.

Laughing, Bob swung down from his horse and hurried over to shake hands with James, Billy, and the others. "Had you boys given up on me?" he asked.

"No, but I must confess to being some worried," James admitted. "You changed horses, I see."

"I had no choice. The Mexicans killed Diablo," Bob said. He looked over at Billy. "Sorry about your horse, Billy. He was a good horse. You might say he saved my life. Even with a bullet in him, he carried me a mile or more, far enough to get away. That's where he keeled over. I had to run the rest of the way on foot."

"You ran all the way to the ranch? That's more than ten miles," James said.

"I know," Bob said. "Believe me, I know."

"Hey," one of the men shouted from the water's edge. "This here is Ramos Garza! You boys killed Garza!"

"Are you sure?" Garrison Cason asked.

"Yeah, I'm sure. I've seen him two or three times."

"Who shot him?" Garrison asked. "Because whoever did, it's worth fifty dollars, far as I'm concerned."

"Then you'd better pay James," Billy said. "He's the one that shot him."

James waved his hand in protest. "Tell you what, Pa. Why don't you give the fifty to Bob? Seems to me like we all owe our lives to him."

"Consider it done," Garrison Cason said. He smiled broadly, his teeth shining brightly in the moonlight.

"Well, thanks," Bob said.

"Don't get too attached to that money, Bob," Billy said. "You're going to spend every penny of it buyin' us drinks in the Oasis."

"Yeah!" one of the other cowboys said.

"It's a deal," Bob agreed, happily.

Chapter Two

The little building stood alone on a country road, ten miles from the nearest town. It had started out as a general store, but because it was the only establishment of trade in this part of the county, its business grew.

As business improved, the building began to expand. One section was added to accommodate a blacksmith shop, the saloon occupied another extension, while a second-story addition provided a hotel. The finished project reflected its hodgepodge origins, the construction spreading out in erratic styles of architecture, mismatched types of wood, and varying shades of paint.

Duke Faglier would have ridden on without giving the place a second notice had he not seen the little splash of color hanging from the saddle of one of the horses standing out front. Duke

19

stopped, tied his horse to the hitching rail, then walked over for a closer look. There was a little strip of cloth tied to the saddle horn and he took it in his hand, examining it closely.

"Oh, it is so beautiful, Duke," Alice had exclaimed as she put the scarf on her head and tied it beneath her chin. "It has so many colors, just like Joseph's coat in the Bible." She pirouetted proudly as she showed off her scarf of many colors.

"It's the prettiest thing I've ever seen," Duke agreed.

The strip of cloth Duke was holding in his fingers at this moment was that same scarf. He had no doubt about it because he had given that scarf to his little sister on her fifteenth birthday.

That was two months ago. Four days ago Duke had returned home to find his mother and father murdered, and his sister dying. Alice lived just long enough to tell of the terrifying evening when a strange man burst into the house while they were eating supper, shot their mother and father, then brutally attacked her.

"Who was he?" Duke had asked. "Who did this? What did he look like?"

"His eye," she gasped. "His eye."

"What about his eye?"

"His eye," she said again, as she drew her last breath.

Duke took the scarf from the saddle, stuck it in his pocket, then went into the building. The inside of the building was dim, a study in light and shadow as bars of sunlight stabbed through the cracks between the boards, illuminating the thousands of dust motes that hung glistening in the air.

Duke stood for a moment just inside the door, studying the layout. To his left was a bar. In front of him were four tables; to the right, a potbellied stove, sitting in a box of sand. Because it was summer the stove was cold, but the stale, acrid smell of last winter's smoke still hung in the air.

One man was behind the bar; a customer was in front. Two men were sitting at one of the tables. A woman was at the back of the room, standing by an upright harpsichord. Her heavily painted face advertised her trade, and she smiled provocatively at Duke as he entered, trying to interest him in the pleasures she had to offer.

Duke stood for a long time without moving. That got everyone's attention, which is exactly what he wanted to do.

"You got somethin' in your craw, mister?" the bartender asked.

"The roan, with the right foreleg stocking," Duke said with a jerk of his head toward the front. "Who's riding him?"

The barkeep, prostitute, and three customers looked at him blankly. No one answered.

Duke pulled his pistol from its holster. "I asked, who is riding him?" When still no one answered, he pointed his pistol toward the barkeep and pulled the hammer back. There was a deadly double click as the sear engaged the cylinder.

"I don't know, mister," the barkeep answered nervously. "I don't pay no attention to what folks are ridin' when they pass through here."

"You, standin' at the bar," Duke said to the customer. "Turn toward me so I can get a good look at you."

The customer looked toward Duke. He had a moon-shaped face and was clean-shaven. His eyes reflected his fright but were otherwise insignificant.

"You two," Duke said to the men at the table. "Look this way. I want to get a good look at your eyes."

"Who are you looking for?" one of the men asked.

"I'll know him when I see him," Duke said. He studied the two men closely, but saw nothing remarkable in their eyes, either.

"Mister, are you looking for a man with a bad eye?" the woman asked.

"There ain't nobody here like that," the bartender said.

"Sure there is, Frank. He's—"

"Marilou, shut your mouth," the bartender

ordered in sharp anger, cutting her off in mid-sentence.

"Mister, I think you had better be the one who keeps quiet," Duke said. "Go ahead, Marilou. What about a man with a bad eye?"

Marilou looked nervously toward the bartender.

"Don't be looking at him, girl. I'm the one you have to satisfy right now," Duke said. "Now, what about this fella with the bad eye?"

"I don't know if he has a bad eye or not, but he has the kind of eyes that never let you know which one of 'em is looking at you," Marilou said.

"Did he ride up here on the horse I asked about?"

"I don't know about that," Marilou said. "But if that horse doesn't belong to any of these gentlemen, then it must be his. He's the only other one in here."

"In here?" Duke asked, sharply, looking around the room again to make certain he hadn't overlooked anyone.

"Marilou, I told you to shut your mouth. This here ain't none of your business!" the bartender said with a growl.

"Mister, I've had about enough out of you," Duke said to the bartender. "Go on, girl. Where is he?"

"Upstairs," Marilou said. "He went upstairs with Kate."

"Thanks."

With his pistol still cocked, and holding it in his crooked arm, muzzle pointing up, Duke started climbing the stairs. He had just reached the top step, when the bartender shouted a warning.

"Frank! Look out! There's someone comin' up for you!"

Surprised that the barkeep would shout a warning, Duke turned to look back downstairs. That was a fortuitous move, for at that very moment the bartender was standing at the bottom of the stairs with a double-barrel shotgun pointing up at him.

"What are you doing, barkeep? This isn't your fight!" Duke shouted.

"Frank's my brother!" the bartender replied, pulling the trigger even as he shouted the words.

Duke managed to jump behind the corner at the top of the stairs just as the bartender fired. The load of buckshot tore a large hole in the door to a room just behind him. Duke stepped back around the corner, then fired at the bartender before he could get off a second shot. His bullet caught the bartender in the neck and he dropped the shotgun, then fell heavily to the floor.

At almost the same moment, four shots sounded from inside one of the rooms. Dust and sawdust flew as four bullets punched holes through the door. Duke flattened himself against the wall, clear of the door. A second later, he heard the sound of crashing window glass.

Without a second thought, Duke ran to the door, kicked it open then dashed into the room. A naked woman on the bed screamed as Duke rushed right by her to the broken window. He leaned through the shattered glass to look down to the ground below. If the man the bartender called Frank had jumped through the window, Duke should still be able to see him.

But Frank had not jumped out. The broken window was a ruse, and Frank was waiting in the corner. With a smile of triumph, he started toward Duke. At that moment Duke sensed someone coming up behind him. He spun around just in time to see a man charging toward him, holding his gun as a club. The man had a ferocious expression on his face, but as the prostitute downstairs had said, it was impossible to tell which of the two glaring eyes was looking at him.

Because Duke turned around in time, he was able to deflect some but not all of Frank's blow. The gun butt missed his head, but it did hit him, with tremendous force, on the shoulder. The crushing blow sent jolts of pain into his neck, his shoulder, and down his arm to the tips of his fingers. The fingers grew numb and he lost his grip on his pistol. The gun slid out of his hand, and he heard it clatter to the floor.

Frank had the advantage of surprise and the momentum of the first blow. Duke went down under his onslaught. With Duke weaponless and flat on his back, Frank put his knee on Duke's chest, then raised his pistol, intending to use it as a club for the killing blow.

Duke's right hand was still numb, but he felt around on the floor with his left hand, trying to find his pistol. Unable to find the pistol, he managed to wrap his fingers around a long shard of glass from the broken windowpane. Reacting quickly, he brought his left hand up, then across, in a slashing motion. The razor-sharp glass shard sliced open Frank's abdomen, disemboweling him. Duke felt Frank's blood and intestines running across his hand. Frank dropped his pistol and put both hands across his belly, trying in vain to stem the flow of blood and spill of intestine.

Duke pushed Frank off of him, then stood up and looked down at him.

"Who are you?" the dying man gasped. "Why did you come after me?"

"My name is Faglier. Does that mean anything to you?"

"Never heard of you."

"What about True and Edna Faglier? What about Alice Faglier? Do you know who they are?"

"No," Frank replied in a strained voice.

"You son of a bitch," Duke said in a low, angry voice. "You murdered my mother, father, and sister, and you don't even know their names." He reached into his shirt and pulled out the scarf of many colors. "Do you remember this? I took it off your saddle."

"Oh yes, now I know who you are talking about," Frank said. He forced a smile. "You know what I think? You won't want to hear this, but that little girl was actually enjoying it. Yes, sir, it was probably a good thing I shot her. She might have grown up to be a whore. You wouldn't have wanted that, would you? A whore for a sister?"

Made angry by Frank's taunting words, Duke picked his pistol up from the floor, pointed it at Frank's head, then cocked it.

"I'm about to close both those bulging bat-eyes of yours for good," Duke said.

"Yes," Frank said. "Yes, shoot me, mister. Don't let me lie here like this."

The barrel of the pistol began shaking as Duke had a battle with himself.

"Shoot me! Shoot me, you bastard!" Frank gasped. "Or do you want to hear me tell you how it was with your sister? How she begged me for it?"

Duke held the pistol for a moment longer, then he found the strength to put it back in the

27

holster. Spitting on Frank, he turned and left the room, even as Frank was screaming at him, begging him to come back and end it.

The bartender's body was lying on the floor at the bottom of the stairs. Although there had been only three customers when Duke arrived, there were at least a dozen there now. No one was holding a weapon, and no one was wearing a badge, but Duke pulled his pistol again, just to be on the safe side.

A couple of men were bent over the bartender.

"Is he dead?" Duke asked, walking over to the bar and pulling a towel off one of the rings. He wrapped the towel around his left hand, which was bleeding, for the shard of glass had cut both ways.

"Yes," one of the men answered.

"I had no quarrel with him. But he left me no choice."

"And Frank?" one of the others asked.

"The girl upstairs can tell you about him," Duke said.

"The sheriff will be wantin' to hold an inquest. You goin' to stick around for that?"

"I don't think so."

"You got witnesses down here that'll testify the bartender shot first. And if the girl upstairs will back you on what happened up there, you got nothin' to worry about."

"I said I'm not staying," Duke repeated. He made a waving motion with his pistol, indicating that everyone should move to one side. "Now, clear a path to the door for me. I've done enough killing for one day. I don't want to kill anyone else, but I will if I have to."

Warily, the men and Marilou moved to one side of the room as Duke started toward the door.

"Mister?" one of the men called.

Duke turned toward him.

"I think maybe you ought to know there's three more of 'em."

"Beg your pardon?"

"Them two you just killed? Frank and Mingus Butrum? Well, they got three more brothers and they ain't likely to take what just happened here lyin' down."

Chapter Three

"It was at a place called Bull Run," Abner Murback was telling the others. "They say it is named after a creek they got there, but I figure it should be called Yankee Run, what with the way all them Union boys skedaddled."

"You reckon this war's goin' to last long enough for us to get into it?" Johnny Parker asked.

"Nah, it'll more'n likely be over in a couple of days," Carl Adams said.

"I don't think so," Abner replied. "What I think Bull Run done is to show the world we're serious about this. There's no doubt in my mind but that there's goin' to be a full-out war now. And when it comes, I aim to be smack dab in the middle of it."

"Ain't goin' to be much of a war," Johnny

30

Parker insisted. "Hell, if the Virginians can do that to Yankees, just think what we Texans could do."

"Yeah, sure wish we had been there," one of the others said.

Abner, Johnny, Carl, and several other young men were in the Oasis Saloon discussing the latest news on what was already being called, by the South, the "War of Northern Aggression," and, by the North, the "War of Rebellion."

"Let's hear it for Texas and the South!" someone shouted, holding up his beer mug. His proposal was greeted by a deep-throated cheer.

"Huzzah!"

"Do you think Bexar County will raise a regiment?" Abner asked.

"Why, we got to get into it now," Carl answered. "We can't let the folks back East win our freedom for us."

"I agree," Johnny said. "If we don't get into this war, ain't no Texan nowhere will be able to hold his head up."

"If Bexar does raise a regiment, who do you think will command it?" Abner asked.

"Far as I'm concerned, there's only one man, and that's Colonel Cason," Carl said.

"Well, yes, you would say that, seein' as you ride for Long Shadow."

"That ain't the only reason I'm sayin' that. Ever'body knows Colonel Cason's got the most experience of anyone. He fought agin the Mexicans in the war for Texas independence, then again when we had to whip 'em a second time."

"And he kind of pulled your bacon out of the fire when we come to rescue you and them others last month against Ramos Garza," Abner said. Abner had been one of the men who rode with Colonel Cason in his rescue party.

"That's for sure," Carl said, good-naturedly.

"Hey, here comes James Cason now," one of the others said. "Wouldn't surprise me none, if ol' James was an officer when we get our regiment formed."

"Well, of course he will be, him bein' the colonel's son an' all," Carl said.

"Yeah, we'll be salutin' him."

"Let's all salute him now, when he comes in," Carl suggested.

Thus it was that when James Cason stepped through the door of the Oasis Saloon, every man inside was standing at attention, rendering their interpretation of a salute.

James was taken back by the demonstration, looking around in surprise.

"Carl, what is all this about?" he asked, taking in the group with a sweep of his hand.

"We're salutin' you," Carl answered.

"I can see that. The question is, why?"

"Well, James, we figured that bein' as you'll

probably be an officer in our regiment, that we may as well get used to it," Carl said.

"What regiment would that be?"

"The one Bexar County will be formin' to go off to fight agin the Yankees," Abner said.

"I see," James said. He looked at all of them, then he stepped up to the bar. "I'll have a beer," he said.

"Ain't you goin' to return our salute, James?" Johnny asked.

James turned toward them and rested his elbows on the bar behind him as the barkeep drew his beer.

"No need to," he said. "I don't plan to be an officer."

"Why not? You didn't fester up none from that wound you got. Hell, you don't even have a limp. And like as not, your pa will be in command of the regiment when it's formed."

"Yeah, and we all agreed he'd want to make his own son an officer."

"Which is fine by us."

"There is no Bexar County regiment that I know of. And if there is one formed, I don't think my pa will agree to command it."

"Why not?"

"Because he doesn't believe in this war, that's why. He doesn't believe in it, and neither do I. I have no intention of going off to fight the Yankees."

There was a look of surprise on the faces of everyone who was gathered in the bar.

"Wait a minute. Are you sayin' you don't want to go to war?"

"That's exactly what I'm saying."

"Well, I'll be damned. I never thought I'd live to see the day a Cason would show the white feather," Abner said.

Abner regretted his words the moment he said them, and they hung over the crowded saloon like the long-lingering peal of a bell that is too loudly rung. Everyone grew quiet as they waited to see what James would do.

"You got no right to say that, Abner," Carl said, defending James. "I've never known a braver man than James Cason. And I ought to know, seein' as how I've seen him in action and you ain't."

James fixed Abner with a cold stare and Abner began to sweat.

Abner ran the back of his hand across his lips. " 'Course," he went on, nervously. "I'm not sayin' that's what I'm seein' now," he said. "The white feather, I mean."

"What, exactly, are you saying?" James asked, as he took a swallow of his beer.

"I'm just sayin' that—well, I ain't never known you, nor no Cason to run from a fight. And I was just wonderin' why it is that you don't want to join the regiment?"

"If it was the Mexicans, or the British, or the French looking to invade our country, I would fight," James answered. "Whether I was made an officer or not, I would fight. But the Yankees? They are our own people—our own kin. My ma and pa both have folks up north—brothers and sisters. I see no reason strong enough to make me take up arms against my own kin."

"It's the principle of the thing," Johnny suggested.

"The principle?"

"Yes. There is such a thing as principle, you know. I mean, that's what makes us men, the fact that we will stand up for principle."

"Johnny's right," several others responded. "It's the principle of the thing."

"Tell me, then, just what principle would we be fighting for?"

"You want to know what we are fightin' for? All right, how about the fact that the Yankees won't let us have our rights?" Abner asked. "That's what we're fightin' for."

"Yeah," the others said. "We're fightin' for our rights."

"Our rights to do what? To own slaves? Let me ask you something, Abner. Just how many slaves do you own?"

"Why, I don't have any slaves, James, you know that," Abner replied.

"And I know Carl doesn't. What about you,

Johnny? Tom? Mitch? Any of you? Do any of you own any slaves?"

"Don't none of us own any slaves, James," Johnny said. "Hell, you know that."

"Yes, I do know it. And neither do I, nor any of my friends, own slaves," James continued. "So here's my question. Why would you be willing to fight in a war where you could get yourself killed, and will for sure be expected to kill others, over a principle that doesn't even affect you?"

"I'll tell you a principle that does affect me," Abner said. "It's seeing all my friends go off to fight in a war, and perhaps die, while I stay here, safe at home."

James took another swallow of his beer, then nodded. "All right, Abner," he finally said. "That is a principle I can understand. If you want to go off and fight in a war because you are guided by your conscience to share the danger with your friends, and not in some youthful quest for glory, I can respect that. But I ask that you show the same respect and understanding for my position. I have no wish to kill my kin. Nor do I want to be killed by them."

"Then, what will you do? Are you just going to stay here in San Antonio and watch the rest of us march off?"

"I don't know the answer to that question,"

James replied. "It is my hope that I never have to find out."

Wilson Creek, Missouri
Friday evening, August 9, 1861:

Outside, the rain drummed against the canvas sides of the tent where General Lyons was making his headquarters. Despite the trench that had been dug around the tent to divert the pooling water, little streams ran across the dirt floor. Duke Faglier, who was acting as a civilian scout for the Union army, was just returning from a patrol behind Confederate lines. Taking his hat off, he poured water from the crown and bent-up brim, before stepping through the opening in the side of the tent to report to the general.

General Lyons, his red hair glowing in the lanternlight, began examining the map as Duke rendered his report.

"And you say they are just north of the Cowskins, Springfield Road?" Lyons asked.

"Yes, sir," Duke replied.

"But it is a feint, correct?"

"No, sir, I don't think so. They are there in strength."

"What is their strength?"

"It could be as high as twenty thousand," Duke answered.

"Damn that Sterling Price," General Lyons

said. "How could he raise such an army so quickly?"

"Well, he is the governor of Missouri, General," his aide explained.

"Former governor," General Lyons replied. Then to Duke, Lyons asked, "Have you eaten?"

"No, sir."

"Lieutenant, have we anything for this man to eat?" Lyons asked his aide.

"I think so, sir," the lieutenant said. Then he continued, "I admit that Price is a former governor, but he is as popular with the people now as he was when he held office. And, outside the city of St. Louis, Missouri is strongly pro-South."

"That is true," General Lyons admitted.

"Here you go, mister," the aide said, then, handing a cloth-wrapped parcel to Duke. When Duke looked up, questioningly, the aide continued. "It's a cold biscuit with a piece of salt pork. Not much, I'm afraid, but it's all we have here."

"Thank you, Lieutenant, this will do just fine," Duke said, unwrapping the biscuit to take a bite.

"Mr. Faglier, you are a Missourian, are you not?" General Lyons inquired.

"I am."

"How is it you are with us, and not with the Rebels?"

"I will admit that it was a hard decision," Duke replied. "I don't want to see the Union dissolved. On the other hand, I'm not happy about fighting against other Missourians. I reckon that's why I decided to serve as a civilian scout, rather than join the army."

"We can't always have what we want," Lyons replied. "But I would be interested in your opinion of General Price's army. Are they to be reckoned with?"

"Yes, sir, I would say so," Duke answered.

"Why? By your own accounts, there is scarcely a modern weapon among the whole lot of them," General Lyons said.

"Well, sir, General Price's army may not be well armed. I mean, they are sitting out there right now with nothing but flintlocks, shotguns, squirrel guns, and some of them with nothing more than Arkansas toothpicks. But they are dangerous."

"Arkansas toothpicks?"

Duke smiled. "It's what we Missourians call knives," he explained.

Lyons snorted. "Knives, on a battlefield. What kind of ragtag army are we facing? Do they actually intend to face us armed with nothing but knives?"

"I wouldn't dismiss those knives out of hand if I were you, General. If the fighting gets to be hand-to-hand, and it probably will, a good man with an Arkansas toothpick is far superior to a soldier trying to use a bayonet."

"Yeah," Lyons agreed. "Yeah, you might be right at that." Lyons walked over to the opening of the tent and stood there, looking out at the rain. "It's still raining."

"Yes, sir," Duke said.

"Somewhere in God's heaven there is an angel with the sole duty of making war miserable, and rain on the battlefield is one of the ways he does it. I suppose that's good, though. If war were all flags and bands and glory, why I reckon man would be at it all the time."

"You think this war is going to last long, General?" Duke asked.

Lyons was silent for a long moment, then he turned toward Duke. The general's eyes were deep and unfathomable.

"Not for me it won't," he said, enigmatically.

Because of the rain, very few people found a dry enough place to sleep that night. Those who did were kept awake by concerns of the upcoming battle.

If Duke had been frightened before the battle, all fear fell away the moment he heard the whine of bullets. He felt only an uncontrollable urge to get into the thick of the fight. There were dead and dying all around him, but they received only a passing thought. As a civilian scout, he was technically a nonbelligerent observer, and he became cool and deliberate, watching the effect of bullets, the showers of bursting shells, and the passage of cannonballs as they cut their murderous channels through the ranks of General Lyons's army.

It quickly became evident that the Rebels were going to carry the day. In a fulfillment of his prophecy of the night before, the war ended for General Lyons when he was killed while leading a charge. During the course of the battle, several other high-ranking officers were killed as well. The sudden loss of their command structure caused all discipline to break down on the battlefield. The Union lines faltered, then began to disintegrate. A gradual withdrawal turned into a full-scale rout as the Rebels swept the Federals from the field.

Duke had no choice but to abandon the field with the others. As he withdrew, a Rebel popped in front of him. Reacting quickly, Duke shot him.

"Duke!" the Rebel soldier yelled in a pained voice as he went down.

Startled to hear the soldier call him by name, Duke ran to the wounded Reb.

"Oh my God! Caleb!" Duke gasped, for the man he had just shot was his younger brother. "I'm sorry!" Duke said. "Forgive me, Caleb! Please, forgive me!"

"It's all right, big brother," Caleb gasped. "You didn't know."

"What, what are you doing here, anyway?" Duke asked. "When did you join the Rebels?"

"I couldn't let this great adventure pass me by," Caleb said. He coughed, and flecks of blood foamed around his mouth.

"I'm going to get help for you," Duke said. He started to stand but Caleb reached up for him and pulled him back down.

"No," he said. "No, it's too late. I'll be dead before you get back."

"Caleb, my God, oh my God!" Duke lamented. "I'm sorry. I'm so sorry."

"It's all right, Duke," Caleb said. "This is what war is."

"Not for me it isn't," Duke insisted. "I had no right to shoot you! I'm not even a soldier!"

Duke looked at his pistol, then with a pained yell, he threw it away, tossing it as far from him as he could. "I don't want any part of this war."

Caleb's breathing was now coming in audible gasps, but he smiled when he heard Duke say that. "Good," he said. "You've got no business in this war, anyway. You are the last one of us now, Duke. Mom, Pop, our sister. Now me. All dead. You are the last one. You have to stay alive for the rest of us."

Duke nodded but said nothing.

"Duke, Duke," Caleb said, reaching up to

clutch him by the arm. "The Butrums. Don't let them find you. I ran across them up in Kansas City. They are a mean bunch. They aim to kill you."

"A lot of people tried to kill me today," Duke said.

"Yes," Caleb replied. "But with the Butrums, it's personal."

Again, Caleb began coughing and gasping. Then, his breathing stopped.

"Caleb? Caleb?" Duke called, but there was no answer.

"Duke, did you mean what you said about quitting the war?" a voice asked.

Startled, Duke looked around to see an old boyhood friend, also in a Rebel uniform.

"Jason, how long have you been standing there?"

"Long enough to watch Caleb die," Jason answered. "I'm sorry."

"I did it," Duke said. "I killed my own brother."

"Like he said, this is war," Jason replied. "Did you mean it? What you said about getting out of the war?"

"Yes," Duke said. "I mean it. I can't fight for the South, but I can't kill any more of my own."

Jason pointed to the southwest. "Go that way," he said. "There are no soldiers in that direction, either our side or yours."

"Thanks, Jason," Duke replied. Standing, Duke took one last look down at Caleb, then he started in the direction Jason had pointed.

"And, Duke . . . ?" Jason called to him.

Duke stopped and looked back.

"Mind what your brother Caleb said about them Butrum boys. They're a mean lot."

Duke nodded, then went on.

Chapter Four

It was just after dark when Duke Faglier rode into San Antonio. From the small adobe houses on the outskirts of town, dim lights flickered through shuttered windows. The kitchens of the houses emitted enticing smells of suppers being cooked, from familiar aromas of fried chicken, to the more exotic and spicy bouquets he couldn't identify.

A dog barked, a ribbony yap that was silenced by a kick or a thrown rock.

A baby cried, a sudden gargle that cracked the air like a bullwhip.

A housewife raised her voice in one of the houses, launching into some private tirade about something, sharing her anger with all that were within earshot.

The downtown part of San Antonio was a

contrast of dark and light. Commercial buildings such as stores and offices were closed and dark, but the saloons and cantinas were brightly lit and they splashed pools of light out onto the sidewalk and into the street. As Duke rode down the road he would pass in and out of those pools of light so that to anyone watching him he would be seen, then unseen, then seen again. The footfalls of his horse made a hollow clumping sound, echoing back from the false-fronted buildings as he passed them by.

By the time he reached the center of town, the night was alive with a cacophony of sound: music from a tinny piano, a strumming guitar, and an off-key vocalist, augmented by the high-pitched laughter of women and the deep guffaw of men. Somewhere in town, a trumpet was playing.

Duke dismounted in front of the Oasis Saloon, tied his horse to the hitching rail, then went inside. Lanterns hanging from overhead wagon wheels emitted enough light to read by, though drifting clouds of tobacco smoke diffused the golden light. He overheard snatches of a dozen or more conversations, many having to do with the war that was being fought back East.

As he stood for a moment just inside the door, Duke happened to see a "pick and switch" operation lift a man's wallet. The victim was a middle-aged man who was leaning over the bar, drinking a beer and enjoying his conversation. While he was thus engaged, a nimble-fingered pickpocket deftly slipped the victim's billfold from his back pocket. Instead of moving away quickly, however, the pickpocket walked slowly and deliberately away from the door, toward the back of the saloon.

Duke watched as the pickpocket passed the pilfered wallet off to an accomplice who was coming in the opposite direction, leaving the saloon. The entire operation was so quick and smooth that the victim never felt a thing. No one else in the saloon saw it happen, and if Duke had not been in the exact spot at the exact time, he wouldn't have seen it, either.

Duke waited until the second man, the one who had received the stolen wallet, passed by him on the way out of the saloon. Then, just as the man got even with him, Duke knocked him down with a well-placed blow to the point of the chin. The pickpocket's accomplice didn't see it coming and he went down and out.

"What the hell!" someone shouted.

"Did you see that?"

The sudden and unexpected incident stopped all conversation as everyone looked toward Duke in disapproval. The barkeep brought a double-barrel shotgun up from under the bar, and though he didn't point it at Duke, it very presence lent some authority to his question.

"You want to tell us what that was all about, mister?" the barkeep asked.

Duke leaned down and reached into the inside jacket pocket of the man he had just knocked out. He pulled out the wallet, then held the wallet out toward the victim.

"I believe this is yours," he said.

In a reflexive action, the victim reached for his back pocket and discovered that it was empty.

"What? I'll be damned!" he said. "That man stole my wallet!" He pointed to the man on the floor who was, at that moment, just beginning to come around.

"No, sir," Duke replied. Duke pointed to the actual pickpocket who was standing at the far end of the bar, now trying to be as inconspicuous as possible. "He is the man who stole your wallet," he said. "This man was just his courier."

The pickpocket tried to run, but two men grabbed him. Two more men took control of the man Duke had knocked down, and the pickpocket and his accomplice were hustled out of the saloon bound for the sheriff's office.

"Mister, I want to thank you," the victim said, extending his hand. "The name is Thornton. Michael Thornton."

"Duke Faglier," Duke said, shaking Thornton's hand.

"Could I buy you a drink, Mr. Faglier?"

"Later perhaps, after I've had my supper," Duke replied. "That is, if a fella can get anything to eat in here," he added to the bartender. "Do you serve food?"

"Steak and potatoes, ham and eggs, your choice," the bartender replied.

"Yes."

"Yes, which?"

"Yes, I'll have steak and potatoes, ham and eggs," Duke said.

Thornton laughed. "The young man is hungry," he said. "Bring him what he wants. I'll pay for it."

"You don't need to buy my supper," Duke said.

"I know I don't need to, son. It's just my way of thanking you."

"If you really want to thank me, you can tell me where a man might find a job in this town."

"You're looking for a job?"

"Yes, sir."

"You aren't afraid of hard work, are you?" Thornton asked.

"Not if it's honest."

"Good enough. I own the livery," Thornton said. "I need a good man, if you are interested."

"I'm interested," Duke said.

"Then the job is yours."

*　　*　　*

Over the next few months after Duke began working at the livery stable, the war continued to be the primary topic of conversation for most of the young men of San Antonio and Bexar County. When Duke was in one of the saloons he often listened, but seldom contributed to the conversations.

The most outspoken of all the young men of the county was Abner Murback. Abner was the son of Tyler Murback. Tyler Murback owned the Circle M Ranch. Second in size only to Long Shadow, the Circle M was a powerful presence in the county, and Abner was a natural leader among his peers.

Tyler had a daughter about James Cason's age. Meg was a beautiful young woman, if a bit spoiled, and Tyler and Garrison Cason entertained hopes that one day their children would marry each other. Everyone expected that marriage to occur some day, and as a result, they were often put together at church socials, picnics, and the like. Even James had accepted the inevitable, but it was not something he dwelled on.

Duke had worked particularly hard this day, and all he wanted was supper and a couple of beers. He had no interest in being drawn into a discussion about the war, but Abner continued to wax poetic and Duke sighed, because he knew there was no way he would be entirely left out.

"Seems to me like we've done showed the Yankees we can whip 'em," Abner Murback was saying, as Duke ordered his supper of pork chops, eggs, fried potatoes, and a beer.

"What I don't understand is why we don't just take us an army into Washington and demand that the Yankees get out of the South and let us alone," Abner continued.

"Yeah," Johnny Parker said. "What do you think about that, Duke?"

If Johnny's question had been an inferred invitation for Duke to join them, he let the invitation slide by, remaining, instead, at his own table, halfway across the barroom floor.

"I don't even think about things like that," Duke called back. "I'm leaving all that up to folks that are a lot smarter than I am."

"They can't be all that damned smart," Billy Swan said. "If they were, we wouldn't be fighting this war in the first place."

"Not fight the war?" Abner replied. "What do you mean, not fight the war? Are you telling me we should just sit back and let the Yankees walk all over us?"

"No Yankee has walked all over me," Billy replied.

"The way I look at it, if a damn Yankee walks

over one Southerner, he walks over every Southerner. Right, Duke?"

Duke held up his hands. "Like I said, Abner, leave me out of it. I don't have any opinions."

Duke had shared with no one his experiences at Wilson Creek.

For a while after the battle at Wilson Creek, there was little to suggest that the war would ever amount to anything more than a series of such skirmishes. For the most part, both sides seemed willing to take a "wait and see" attitude. Under such conditions, there was little need to increase the size of the army. The closest any of the young men of Bexar County got to the war, was to read the latest reports in the newspapers.

In answer to the call from the governor of Texas and the President of the Confederate States of America, Bexar County raised a regiment. It was commanded not by Garrison Cason as everyone had predicted, but by Colonel Nelson Culpepper, a career soldier who had resigned from the United States Army shortly after the war began.

At the last moment James almost had a change of heart. Despite his protestations against the war, he was nearly caught up in the sweep and pageantry of the thing. Bands played, and flags and pennants snapped in the breeze as the "Bexar County Fusiliers" formed ranks in the town plaza. Pretty girls and weeping mothers stood along the edge of the street, waving silken handkerchiefs at their brave men, already heroes even though they had yet to hear a shot fired in anger. Beneath the tunics of more than one soldier was the pressed flower given to him at the going away cotillion held the night before. In some cases, more than one soldier carried flowers given to them by the same girl. In other cases, some of the soldiers were carrying the flowers of more than one girl.

The farewell speeches had been given and the men were drawn up in parade formation, ready for the order to move out. Colonel Culpepper, the most splendid-looking man of all in his gray-and-gold uniform, was the only one mounted, sitting importantly on a prancing white charger. Holding a flashing saber up in the morning sunlight, he gave the command that moved the regiment out.

"Bexar Fusiliers!" he shouted, calling out the preparatory command.

"Battalion!"

"Company!"

The supplementary commands echoed up and down the long formation.

"Forward!"

Again, the supplementary commands echoed from the battalion and company commanders.

"Forward!"

"March!" Colonel Culpepper finished with the command of execution.

The drums began the marching cadence as the regiment moved out. Their departure was met with cheers and applause, sprinkled here and there with last-minute good-byes as families called out to their loved ones by name.

"Bye, Carl, Joe, Syl!"

"You be careful, Abner!"

"George, you write to me!"

"Kill lots of Yankees, Tommy!" The last was from a younger brother, and it caused titters of laughter to ripple through the ranks.

"Now, Tommy, don't you go an' kill all them Yankees. You save some of 'em for us," Syl teased, and Tommy the young soldier flushed in embarrassment.

"Yeah, we don't want you gettin' all the glory for yourself," Carl added.

"Quiet in the ranks," one of the officers ordered.

Within ten more minutes, the regiment could no longer be seen, though it could still be heard. The rhythmic beat and roll of distant drums and the measured cadence of shuffling feet lingered over Military Plaza.

Every able-bodied cowboy employed by Long Shadow had marched out with the regiment, leaving the ranch without any hands to run the place. Despite that, James continued to feel a twinge of regret for not having gone himself, though the twinge wasn't strong enough to make him change his mind. He crossed the plaza, considered going into a cantina, but chose the saloon instead.

Chapter Five

Near Corinth, Mississippi
Friday, April 4, 1862:

Colonel Nelson Culpepper and his eager but as yet untested Bexar County Fusiliers reached Corinth, Mississippi, on the fourth of April. The Texans were but a small part of a growing Confederate army just south of the Mississippi-Tennessee border. Arriving almost simultaneously with the Bexar County Fusiliers was General Braxton Bragg and his ten thousand battle-proved veterans. In addition, the governors of several Confederate states had answered Johnston's call to provide more men, so that the army grew to an even greater size. The commanding general of all the Confederate forces in the field at Corinth was General Albert Sidney Johnston.

Just across the border, in Tennessee, the

Union army, under General Ulysses Grant, was also collecting troops for what was shaping up to be the biggest battle of the war thus far.

Giving his men permission to rest in place, Colonel Culpepper reported to General Johnston.

"Colonel Culpepper, I am pleased to see you," General Johnston said, greeting the colonel. "You wouldn't have any information on the whereabouts of General Price, would you?"

"No, sir, I'm afraid I don't," Culpepper replied. "We came here directly from San Antonio, Texas."

Johnston stroked his cheek and nodded. "Yes, and you are very welcome. I just hoped that, by chance encounter, you might have some news. The addition of General Price and his Missourians would ensure us victory here."

"General, don't overlook the fact that these men are Texans," Colonel Culpepper said, loudly enough for his men to hear and respond with a cheer. "I think we will more than compensate for any Missourians that don't show."

Johnston smiled, then nodded. "I'm sure they will," he said.

"Where do you want us, General?"

"You will be under my direct command," Johnston said.

"Thank you, sir. I consider that an honor."

"Do you have an aide, Colonel?"

"I don't have an aide, sir, but I do have an orderly. Private Abner Murback."

"Is he a good man?"

"Yes, sir, he is a very good man."

"If you wouldn't mind, I wonder if you would attach him to me temporarily," Johnston said. "My aide has taken ill and returned to Jackson yesterday."

"Well, yes, sir, I suppose I could," Colonel Culpepper said. "But then you would have a private for an aide, and you are a general, sir."

"You say Murback is a good man. Would he make a good officer?"

"Yes, sir, I suppose he would."

"Then, if you recommend it, I will promote him to second lieutenant."

"I would be glad to recommend it, but we already have a full complement of officers in the regiment."

"I'll carry his commission against my staff, that way it won't reflect upon your regimental complement."

"Very good, sir," Culpepper said. "Murback!" he called.

Abner, who had been seeing to the colonel's horse, hurried up when he was called.

"Lieutenant, you will be attached to my staff until further notice," General Johnston said.

"Lieutenant?" Abner replied.

"Yes. I've just given you a commission."

Abner smiled broadly, then came to attention and saluted the general. "Yes, sir!" he said. "Thank you, sir."

After the brief meeting with Culpepper, Johnston left, signaling Abner to come with him. With good-natured teasing and catcalls from his old regiment, Abner left Colonel Culpepper and his fellow Texans, to follow General Johnston.

"General, uh, exactly what does an aide do?" Abner asked.

"It's a pretty simple job, Murback," Johnston replied. "You just do what I tell you to do. Do you think you can handle that?"

Abner laughed. "Yes, sir, well, I have a lot of experience doing that, so I reckon I'm your man all right."

Abner followed General Johnston into a large and elegant two-story farmhouse that was being used as his headquarters.

"Are you hungry?" Johnston asked.

"Yes, sir, a little. We were about to have supper."

"Well, you'll be messing with the headquarters staff now," Johnston said. He nodded toward the kitchen. "I think there is some cold chicken left, and some coffee. You are welcome to it."

"Thank you, General," Abner replied. He walked into the kitchen and started to pull back a cloth that was draped over the food on the table.

"Here, Private, what are you doing there?" a sergeant asked, harshly.

Overhearing the remark, Johnston stuck his head back in the kitchen. "Cooper, this is Lieutenant Murback. He is acting as my aide-de-camp. See if you can find a lieutenant's blouse for him."

"Yes, sir," the sergeant said. "I beg your pardon, sir," he added to Abner.

Abner, unused to being called sir, smiled. "That's quite all right, Sergeant Cooper," he replied. He pointed to the table. "Is it all right if I get something to eat now?"

"Yes, sir, indeed it is, sir," the sergeant said. "Would the lieutenant like some coffee?"

"Yes, thank you," Abner replied. Abner turned back the cloth and selected a drumstick. He had just taken a bite when he heard a commotion in the living room of the house. He nodded toward the sound. "What's going on out there?"

"The general has called all the other generals to a meeting," the sergeant said. "I don't know what it's about, though, because I didn't get invited." The sergeant laughed at his own joke.

"Well, I didn't, either, but I think I'll just take a peek," Abner said.

Holding his coffee cup in one hand and his

piece of chicken in the other, Abner stepped into the open door frame, then stood there, just out of the way, watching as Generals Beauregard, Bragg, Polk, Hardee, and Breckinridge attended General Johnston's conference.

There were not enough places for all the generals and their executive officers to sit, so Beauregard, who was second in command only to Johnston, disdained a chair or a place on the sofa, to sit on the floor near the fireplace. When several officers of lesser rank offered their own seats, Beauregard waved them off, insisting that he was quite comfortable where he was.

"Gentlemen," Johnston said when all were assembled, "while I have guarded against an uncertain offensive, I am now of the opinion that we should entice the enemy into an engagement as soon as possible, before he can further increase his numbers."

"General, I think we should strike at Pittsburg Landing right now, while the Yankees are engaged in off-loading their boats," Bragg suggested. "They haven't built any fortifications, and my scouts tell me they've set up tents, just as if they were on parade."

"An attack of the kind you propose is exactly what the Yankees are counting on," Beauregard said.

"What do you mean?" Bragg asked.

"Think about it, Braxton," Beauregard replied.

"Why are they setting up tents? Why have they built no fortifications? Because they are hoping to draw us out in a bold and foolish attack."

"Do you think boldness is inappropriate?" General Johnston asked.

"Not at all, General," Beauregard replied. "But I think boldness should be tempered with caution. I prefer a defensive offense."

"You talk in riddles, sir," Bragg said, and the other generals laughed.

"Yes, General, perhaps you would share with us what you mean," Johnston said.

Beauregard stood up, brushed off the back of his trousers, and cleared his throat. "I think we should take up a position that would compel the enemy to develop his intentions to attack us. Then, when he is within striking distance of us, we should go on the offensive and crush him, cutting him off, if possible, from his base of operations at the river. If we could then force a surrender from such a large army, the North would have no choice but to sue for peace. We could win the entire war, right here, right now."

The others all began speaking at once, and Johnston had to hold up his hand to quiet them.

"Gentlemen, gentlemen, I appreciate your suggestions and ideas, but as I am in command here, the ultimate responsibility rests with me. General Beauregard, your contention that we could win the war right here is a good one. That is why we must not let the opportunity slip out of our grasp. But I believe General Bragg's suggestion offers us the greatest chance for success. I believe it is imperative that we strike now, before the enemy's rear gets up from Nashville. We have him divided, and we should keep him so if we can."

Johnston's word was final, so there was no further argument on that subject. The discussion then turned to the plan of battle, and in this, Johnston decided to form the army into three parallel lines, the distance between the lines to be one thousand yards. Hardee's corps was to form the first line, Bragg's the second. The third would be composed of Polk on the left and Breckinridge on the right.

"As second in command, General Beauregard will coordinate your efforts. Gentlemen, please have your elements in position by seven o'clock in the morning. We shall begin the attack at eight."

There was a buzz of excited conversation as, for a few moments, the generals discussed the orders with each other.

"And now, I am certain that you all have staff meetings to conduct, so I release you to return to your units," Johnston said by way of dismissal.

The assembled officers stood and saluted as one. Then they trooped outside, clumped across the porch, and mounted their horses to return to their units. Beauregard stayed behind.

Abner had watched it all from his position in the doorway, so fascinated by being a witness to the actual battle plans that he forgot all about being hungry. His half-eaten piece of chicken was still in his hand, and the coffee in his cup was getting cool.

Johnston stayed in the front door for a long time after the others left. He hung his head, almost as if praying, and during that time Beauregard said nothing. The only sound in the room was the popping and snapping of the wood fire burning briskly in the fireplace.

"Excuse me, sir," the sergeant said quietly, and Abner stepped out of the way as Sergeant Cooper, carrying coffee, moved into the living room to give each of the generals a fresh cup.

"Thank you, Sergeant," General Beauregard said.

The sergeant left and Abner realized that he, too, should leave. After all, this was a private moment between the two top commanders in the field. Yet it was that very thing, the fact that he was an observer to such a private moment, that kept him glued to his position in the doorway. His presence was either not noticed, or was unobtrusive enough to cause no problem, for neither Johnston nor Beauregard indicated that he should leave.

The coffee was hot, and Johnston sucked it noisily through extended lips.

"Gus, I've drunk coffee around hundreds of fires on dozens of campaigns over the years, but I tell you now, tomorrow will be my last," Johnston finally said.

Beauregard looked up with a startled expression on his face. "Why, General, whatever do you mean?"

"I fear I will not survive the battle tomorrow."

General Beauregard tried to dismiss Johnston's statement with a laugh. "General, you've been in battle before. You know that every man, be he general or private, feels fear."

Johnston shook his head. "No, you don't understand. The funny thing is, I have no fear. I am certain that I shall be killed, and with that certainty has come the biblical 'peace that surpasseth all understanding.' I can't explain it to you, Gus. It is something you must feel, though you can't feel it until you are facing the same situation."

"But you can't know with a certainty," Beauregard argued. "The hour of his death is known to no man."

"Until it is upon you, Gus. Then you know. Then you know," Johnston repeated quietly, as if talking to himself.

Beauregard made no further efforts to dissuade General Johnston. Instead he just put down his coffee and left quietly by the front door. Abner felt now that he, too, was somehow intruding upon a very private moment, so he turned and walked back into the kitchen, leaving General Albert Sidney Johnston alone with his thoughts.

"Sergeant Cooper, where does the general's aide sleep?" he asked.

"He generally just finds a place, Lieutenant," Sergeant Cooper said. He pointed to one corner of the kitchen. "If I was you, I'd just throw down a bedroll over there."

"Thanks, I guess I will," Abner said.

As Johnston's army maneuvered into position early the next morning, an abrupt April thunderstorm broke over the winding columns. The rain filled hat brims, flowed down the soldiers' backs, and drummed into puddles on the dirt trails. Wagon and artillery wheels cut through rain-soaked roads, turning them into muddy quagmires that caked up on the wheels and gathered in great mud balls on the shoes of the marching soldiers, making every inch of progress most difficult. The army moved, when it moved at all, in jerky, halting operations. Periodically they would stop for long periods of time while the men stood, made miserable by the falling rain. Then the army would lurch into movement that would inevitably cause the trailing columns to have to break into a difficult and exhausting trot just to keep up.

Scattered on both sides of the road during all this were the discarded items of soldiers on the march: overcoats, shovels, rain-soaked playing cards, letters, newspapers, and even Bibles.

Finally the army was called to a halt so that General Johnston's orders, which by now had been transcribed into a score or more copies, could be read to the various regiments. Abner had delivered a copy to Colonel Culpepper and he stood in the rain with the others listening, as Culpepper read them aloud, shielding the orders from the rain by holding his hat over the piece of paper on which they were written.

"Soldiers of the Army of the Mississippi," the colonel read. Then clearing his voice, he moved into the body of the orders:

"I have put into motion to offer battle to the invaders of your country. With the resolution and disciplined valor becoming men fighting, as you are, for all worth living and dying for, you can but march to a decisive victory over the agrarian mercenaries sent to subjugate and despoil you of your liberties, property, and honor. Remember the precious stake involved; remember the dependence of your mothers, your wives, your sisters, and your children on the result; remember the fair, broad, abounding land, the happy homes, and the ties that would be desolated by your defeat.

"The eyes and hopes of eight millions of people rest upon you. You are expected to show yourselves worthy of your race and lineage, worthy of the women of the South, whose noble devotion in the war has never been exceeded in any time. With such incentives to brave deeds, and with the trust that God is with us, your generals will lead you confidently to the combat, assured of success."

After finishing reading, the colonel looked up. "And it is signed by A.S. Johnston, General."

"Hip, hip!" someone shouted.

"Hoorah!" his call was answered.

Having delivered the orders to the commanding officer of his old regiment, Abner exchanged a few pleasantries with his friends and returned to General Johnston's headquarters.

Although it had been General Johnston's intention to have the men in position by seven and begin the attack by eight, eight o'clock came and passed with the Southern columns still bogged down in the stop-and-go marching that had thus far marked their progress on the muddy arteries that were the roads.

General Bragg, a West Point graduate and hero of the Mexican War, was beside himself with consternation. One of his divisions was lost somewhere in the rain on the jammed, muddy roads, and the lateness of his corps was causing the entire operation to dissolve.

Beauregard was riding him mercilessly, and though Bragg had done everything within his power to keep to the schedule, he made no excuses to General Beauregard because he knew that the ultimate responsibility lay with the commander. And as Bragg must suffer the tirade from Beauregard, so too would Beauregard hear from Johnston, who, in turn, was ultimately responsible to the governors of Tennessee, Mississippi, and Alabama, as well as to Jefferson Davis and the Confederate Congress.

As the men began reaching their positions, the sun finally came out. By the time it made its first appearance, however, it was already high in the sky, for the eight o'clock deadline had long since passed. The men, fearful that the rain may have dampened the powder in their rifles, began testing the powder by snapping the triggers. As a result, all up and down the line their muskets popped and banged, well within earshot of the Union outposts.

In addition, the untrained and untested men who made up the Confederated army had their spirits so invigorated by the warming sun that, excited at the prospect of the battle and glory that lay before them, they began giving a series of Rebel yells. Some started shooting rabbits and doves to cook for their lunch, justifiable in their minds because most had eaten their three days' of rations in the first day.

For two more dragging hours, Generals Johnston and Beauregard stood by as Bragg continued to bring up his corps. By now the sun was straight overhead, but the rear division was still nowhere to be seen.

"General Bragg," General Johnston said, "we are waiting."

"Yes, sir. I'm sorry, sir."

"Where is your division?"

"I'm not certain, General," Bragg said. He pointed south. "It's back there, somewhere. The mud, the crowded roads . . ." He stopped in midsentence. Since the others had had to put up with the same conditions, the excuse sounded feeble, even to his own ears.

General Johnston took out his watch and looked at it.

"It is twelve-thirty," he said. He snapped the watch shut and put it back in his pocket. "This is perfectly puerile! This is not war!"

It took two more hours for Bragg's lost division to come up front, and two more hours beyond that for it to be put into position. By that time it was four-thirty in the afternoon and the shadows were growing longer.

Suddenly there was the unmistakeable sound

of a drummer giving the long roll. General Beauregard put his hand to his head in consternation. "Is there to be no respite from the bungling?"

Looking around, he saw Abner.

"Lieutenant Murback, would you please find the idiot who is beating that drum and silence him?" he commanded.

"Yes, sir," Abner replied.

Once mounted, Abner rode down the line toward the sound of the beating drum. When he reached a point quite near it, he stopped and summoned a sergeant.

"Sergeant, I want you to find whoever is banging on that drum and have it stopped at once," he ordered.

To his surprise, the sergeant, and several of the men around him laughed.

"What is so funny?" Abner asked, irritated at the unexpected response.

"Don't rightly know how I'm goin' to get that drum stopped, Lieutenant," the sergeant replied. "Seein' as it's over to the Yankee camp."

"The Yankee camp?"

"Yes, sir. I can walk over there'n tell the little feller to stop, but like as not he won't pay no attention to me," the sergeant joked, and again the men laughed.

"Never mind, Sergeant," Abner said, laughing with him. He looked across the woods toward the sound of the drum. "I doubt he would even pay attention to General Beauregard. Very well, men, carry on as you were."

"Yes, sir," the sergeant said, still smiling at the joke.

Abner returned to General Beauregard to give him the news that they were listening to a Yankee drum.

"Well, that does it, then," Beauregard said. "If we can hear them, there's no doubt they have heard us."

General Johnston was speaking with General Polk. Polk had been Johnston's roommate at West Point. More recently he had been ordained an Episcopal bishop; as a result, he was referred to as "the Bishop" fully as often as he was called General.

"There is no longer any chance of surprise. By now the Yankees will be entrenched up to their ears," Beauregard said.

"So, what are you telling me, Gus?" Johnston asked.

"I'm suggesting that you might want to reconsider the attack order, General. Perhaps we would be better served by withdrawing to Corinth to strengthen our own defenses and let the Yankees bring the fight to us."

"No, no, I strongly disagree," General Polk said. "Our troops are most eager for battle. Consider this, gentlemen. They left Corinth to fight, and if they don't fight, they will be as demoralized as if they had been whipped."

"I totally agree," General Bragg said. "We can't even consider withdrawal now."

"Funny you should say that, General Bragg, as it was your delay that has put us into this situation," Beauregard reminded him.

"I apologize for the disruption in plans my corps caused," Bragg said. "I make no excuses, but I do apologize."

General Breckinridge rode into camp then and, when he dismounted, was surprised to learn that the impromptu war council he had happened upon was even contemplating withdrawal.

"What is your opinion, General?" Johnston asked Breckinridge after outlining the situation for him.

"Gentlemen, I say we attack. Speaking for myself, I would as soon be defeated as retire from the field without a fight."

"Well, that leaves us only Hardee to hear from," Beauregard said.

Breckinridge chuckled. "Hell, Gus, you know where Bill stands on this. He's already deployed and eager for battle. If he were here, he would vote to attack."

"Then it looks to me as if the vote is in," Jonshton said, "and there's no doubt as to the way it has gone. The attack is still on."

"Now? With darkness nearly upon us?" Beauregard asked. "Do you intend to launch a night attack?"

"No, we would have no means of control during such an attack. We will go at first light tomorrow," Johnston said. "Gentlemen, once all your troops are in position, put them at ease and have them sleep on their arms in line of battle. At least tomorrow we will have no unexpected delays in arrival."

"General, there is one more thing you should consider," Beauregard said, not yet ready to give up his argument.

"What is that?" Johnston asked.

"General Buell," Beauregard said, referring to the Union general arriving from Nashville. "He has, in all likelihood, joined with the others by now, and if so, that would bring the number of men arrayed against us to nearly seventy thousand or more."

"The attack order stands," Johnston replied.

"Very good, sir. I will see that everyone gets the word," Beauregard said. The decision having been made, Beauregard was, once more, the loyal subordinate.

Beauregard and the other generals left to attend to their various duties. Johnston watched them ride away, then he turned to Abner, who had listened with great interest to the entire discussion. Abner could see the look of determination in General Johnston's eyes.

"You were listening to our conversation?" Johnston asked Abner.

"Yes, General."

"You understand, don't you, Lieutenant Murback? We have no choice but to attack. We have given away too much ground as it is, and now the Yankees are on our very doorstep. If we don't stop them here, they will occupy all of the South within six months including . . . where is it you are from? Texas?"

"Yes, sir. Bexar County, Texas."

"Then you understand why we must stop them here. General Beauregard is worried because their numbers may be seventy thousand? Hell, I would attack if they were a million." He was silent for a moment longer, then, inexplicably, he chuckled. "But don't worry, my young friend. Ultimately, the numbers are unimportant. Like us, the Yankees are spread out between Lick Creek and Owl Creek, and they can present no greater front between those two creeks than we can. In fact, the more men they crowd in there, the more difficult it would be for them to maneuver, and the worse we can make it for them."

Johnston was silent for a long moment, then he looked at Abner. "All the boys from your county came, I suppose?"

"No, sir," Abner said. "We had some who stayed back, some of my closest friends in fact. They're not cowards, either, because I've seen them fight against Mexicans and outlaws. It's just that, they say they don't believe in this war."

"But you came," Johnston said. "You believe in this war?"

"I don't know if I can answer that question, General. If I thought I was just fighting so rich men could keep their slaves, why, I don't think I would be here, either. I think it's more than that, maybe something like honor and duty, and love of one's land. It's more complicated than I can understand, but . . . here I am."

"Were there bands playing, flags flying, and pretty girls waving when you left?" Johnston asked.

Abner grinned broadly. "Yes, sir, there surely was that," he said proudly.

"I'm glad," Johnston said. He was quiet for a long moment before he spoke again. "After this battle, the country's mood is going to change. Never again will men go off to war with bands playing, flags waving, and women throwing flowers at marching troops. We are in for a day or two of bloodletting the likes of which this nation has never seen. It will change our way of looking at war forever."

Johnston wandered off several steps, and Abner knew that he wanted to be by himself. Respecting the general's need for privacy, Abner pulled some cold jerky from his saddlebag, walked over to an exposed root, and sat down to have his supper.

Chapter Six

San Antonio, Texas
Saturday, April 5, 1862:

The Oasis was much less crowded now than it had been before the regiment left. That was understandable since business had been exceptionally good over the last several weeks. Young men had come, not only from the surrounding ranches, but also from all over Texas to be a part of the regiment. Consequently, as the regiment was forming, the new recruits spent many evenings in the saloon, talking loudly of deeds of daring as yet undone.

With the departure of the regiment, most of the saloon's customers were gone. There remained only those men who were too old to serve, and a few young men who, for one reason or another, had refused to go with the others.

On this particular day, four of the young men who did not leave with the regiment were sitting around a table in the Oasis Saloon. The four were James Cason, Bob Ferguson, Billy Swan, and Duke Faglier. Although Duke had arrived in San Antonio only a few months earlier, he had already formed a friendship with James, Bob, and Billy.

Nobody knew much about Duke, for he was a very quiet-spoken young man. James was curious about his new friend's past, but would never presume to question him.

"Has anyone heard from the regiment?" Billy Swan asked.

"Pa said that Mr. Murback got a letter from Abner," James said. "The letter came from somewhere in Louisiana."

"Are they fightin' in Louisiana?" Bob asked.

"According to the letter they hadn't seen any fighting yet. They were just marching every day. He said he thought they might be going up to Tennessee."

The men were silent for a long moment, then James spoke again.

"This is turning out to be a lot harder than I thought it would be," James admitted.

"What is?" Bob asked.

"Staying behind while all our friends have gone to war. Knowing that they are facing dangers while we are safe at home."

"You aren't having second thoughts, are you?" Bob asked.

"I don't like the way others look at us, or

what they think of of us. And I don't fault them for their opinions. But as for the war? No, I'm not having second thoughts. No good can come of this war, and I don't want to have anything to do with it."

"I agree that no good can come of this war," Bob said. "But I must confess that I feel a little like you. I feel guilty about being at home while all the others our age, and some much older, are doing our fighting for us."

"That's just it, though," James said. "I don't really feel that they are fighting for me. This isn't my cause."

"True. But it is our state. Also, there is something to be said for the glory of battle."

"There *is* no glory in battle," Duke said, emphatically. It was his first comment on the subject, and he punctuated his statement with a swallow of his beer.

In the few months the others had known him, this was the most resolute statement Duke had ever made.

"Oh, come, Duke, are you saying you weren't just a little stirred by the flags and drums and excitement?" Billy asked. "I don't have any personal stake in this war, but I would be lying if I said I had absolutely no desire to test myself on the battlefield."

"Your first test would be to keep from soiling your britches," Duke said.

"Wait a minute!" Billy bristled. "Are you saying I would be afraid?"

"That's not what I mean by soiling your britches. It's just that by the time the fighting starts, nearly everyone is suffering from camp diarrhea, and many a man embarrasses himself when the shooting begins. But yes, I'm sure you would be afraid. Although I've only known you a short time, you don't strike me as a fool, Billy Swan, and anyone who isn't afraid is a fool."

The others were quiet, giving way to Duke's observations. He continued.

"Then, when the fighting does start, you feel completely alone, even though you are in the middle of thousands of men. You think that every bullet, every exploding shell, every cannonball is coming straight for you.

"But you learn you aren't the only target when you have to step over the dead and dying; men lying on the ground with their guts spilling in the dirt, or with bloody stumps twitching uncontrollably where arms and legs once were. Finally, you realize that all the dead on that field are the same. It doesn't matter whether they are Yanks or Rebs, they all speak the same language, pray to the same God, and die in the same mortal agony. They are your neighbors, friends"—Duke paused for a moment before he added softly—"and brothers."

Duke took a swallow of his beer, then wiped

his mouth with the back of his hand, knowing that he had the complete attention of the others. "No, my friends," he finished. "There is no glory in battle. And believe me, any guilt you may have about avoiding that madness is misplaced."

James, Bob, and Billy were totally shocked by the intensity of Duke's comments. But if they were waiting on him to elaborate, they were disappointed, because he said nothing else.

"So, you reckon Abner is going through all that, now?" Bob asked.

"I reckon he is," James said. He held up his glass. "To Abner," he said.

"And to everyone else caught up in this war," Duke added.

They drank the toast, then James sighed. "I agree with everything you said, Duke. Still, it's going to be hard to hang around here and face our neighbors. And as the war goes on, it's going to be even harder."

"It won't be hard if we aren't here," Billy suggested.

"If we aren't here? What do you mean? Are you suggesting that we should go somewhere?"

"Yep," Billy replied.

"Where?"

"Dakota Territory."

"Why do you want to go there?"

Billy smiled, clasped his hands together, put

his elbows on the table and leaned forward. "Gold," he said, simply.

"Gold?"

"I got the news from a whiskey drummer this morning," Billy said. "They've recently discovered gold in the Dakota Territory. They say it's as big a strike as what happened in California a few years ago. Only thing is, the whole country is so caught up in this war that hardly nobody is paying attention to it."

"If that is true—" James started.

"It is true," Billy interrupted. "The drummer swears to it. In fact, he said he was giving up his sales job and was going up to Dakota himself."

"What do you think, James?" Bob asked. "You think maybe we ought to go up there and have a look around?"

"Well, if you want my opinion," Duke said before James could answer, "I think we would be fools not to. Think of how many people got rich out of the California strike, and who knows how many went out there. If everyone back here is caught up in the war, there won't be that many people out there. That means our chances of getting a piece of that gold pie would be much better. And more importantly, the fewer the people, the larger that piece of pie will be."

"What do you say, James?" Bob asked again, his voice now hopeful.

Though no one had elected James to the position, he was the unquestioned leader of the little group and everyone waited now to see what his response would be. They knew that, without his support, the adventure would be stillborn.

James smiled broadly. "I say let's do it," he said.

"Yeah!" Bob said, and the boys laughed and shook hands as they contemplated what lay before them.

"Lord, wouldn't Abner like to go with us, though?" James said.

Corinth, Mississippi
April 5, 1862:

Though the day had begun with rain, it was ending now with a clear, red sunset, shining through oaks that were green with new growth. The moon, in crescent, rose in a dark blue twilight, then, finally, the sky darkened and the stars came out.

Standing out on the porch of the house, Abner could hear faint bugle calls in the distance, and he looked toward the dark woods that separated the two armies. On the other side of the woods was the enemy. There, men dressed in blue were bedding down for one last night before the killing began.

Whippoorwills called from the woods, and as

Abner looked out across the field where the Confederate army was bivouacked he could see the glow of campfires around which men in gray, sharing the same language, culture, religion, history, and, in some cases, family as those in blue, waited for the events of tomorrow.

Abner thought about what General Johnston had said with regard to the great bloodletting that was about to take place, then he thought about James Cason, Bob Ferguson, and Billy Swan, back home in Texas. They refused to come to war because they didn't want to kill their own kin, or be killed by their own.

Abner had a first cousin who lived in Illinois. Cephus Murback was the son of Abner's father's brother. Cephus and Abner were within a few weeks of being the same age; they were of the same name and same blood. Was Cephus on the other side of the line tonight? Could it be possible that, tomorrow, he would kill one of his own kin? Or be killed by one of his own kin?

"God," Abner prayed under his breath. "How have we let it all come to this?"

The next morning, on Sunday, April 6, 1862, on the Mississippi-Tennessee border, near a small church meeting house called Shiloh, General Johnston commenced the battle that would, ever after, bear the name of the little meeting house.

The attack met with immediate, initial success as the Union lines sagged and crumpled and Union troops fled to safety under the bluff along the river. A few brave Union soldiers held on at a place called the "Hornet's Nest," though at a terrible cost in terms of lives lost.

The Shiloh campground had been General Sherman's place of bivouac during the night before, but now General Beauregard made the little log church his personal headquarters. From it, he issued orders and dispatched reinforcements where they were needed, thus affording General Johnston the freedom to move up and down the line of battle, giving encouragement to the men.

Abner was with Johnston, who was at that moment on the extreme right end of the battle line. To those who needed a calming influence, Johnston spoke quietly. "Easy, men, make every shot count. Keep calm, don't let the Yankees get you riled."

To those he felt needed more spirit, he injected a note of ferocity to his words: "Men of Arkansas, you are skilled with the Arkansas toothpick, let us use that skill with a nobler weapon, the bayonet. Use it for your country! Use it for your state! Use it for your fellow soldiers! Use it well!"

General Johnston was well mounted on a large, beautiful horse, and his presence among the men, whether he was speaking or not, was all the inspiration they needed. His progress along the line could be followed easily through the rippling effect of hurrahs shouted by the soldiers.

"Hey! Lookie here!" a soldier shouted as they came across what had been a Yankee camp. "These damn Yankees left their food still a-cookin'!"

"Yahoo!" another shouted, and to Abner's surprise and frustration, nearly half the army broke off its pursuit of the fleeing Union soldiers to sit down and eat the breakfast the Yankees had so recently abandoned.

"You men!" Abner shouted. "Leave that be! We've got the Yankees on the run! Let's finish the job, then you can come back to it!"

"Are you kiddin'? There won't be nothin' left," a corporal said, grabbing a couple of biscuits and a hunk of salt pork.

"Lieutenant, let the stragglers be," General Johnston shouted to Abner. "We have more important things to do! We're losing cohesion here!"

Abner could see what Johnston was talking about. The underbrush, gullies, twisting roads, and pockets of stiff Union resistance had disrupted the orderly progress of the attack. The three lines of battle, so carefully sketched out on the battle map, had become terribly disjointed.

Divisions, brigades, and regiments became so intermingled that men found themselves fighting side-by-side with strangers and listening to commands given by officers they didn't even know. Over it all was the cacophonous roar of battle: thundering cannon, booming muskets, shrieking shells, screams of rage, curses of defiance, fear, and pain, the whole enshrouded in a thick, opaque cloud of noxious gun smoke.

"Lieutenant Murback, get back to Beauregard as quickly as you can. Tell him I wish to reorganize into four sections, Hardee and Polk on the left, Bragg and Breckinridge on the right!"

"Yes, sir," Abner replied. "Where will you be, General?"

"I? I will be here, right in front of this . . . this hornet's nest," Johnston said, referring to the ferocious fighting that was going on in front of them.

Abner galloped back to Shiloh Church. Some of the wounded had straggled back as far as the church and many were sitting or lying around on the ground, attended to by doctors and their orderlies. Beauregard was in conversation with two colonels when Abner reported to him.

"General Johnston's compliments, sir," Abner said, saluting.

"Yes, yes, what is it, Lieutenant?" Beauregard asked, obviously displeased at being interrupted during this critical time.

"The general wishes you to reorganize into four sections, Hardee and Polk on the left, Bragg and Breckinridge on the right."

"Reorganize in the midst of battle?" Beauregard replied. "And how am I supposed to do that, did the general say?"

Abner shook his head. "I'm sorry, General, he didn't say. He just said to reorganize into four—"

"—Sections, Hardee and Polk and the left, Bragg and Breckinridge on the right—yes, yes, I heard that," Beauregard said. Sighing, he stroked his Vandyke beard, then looked at the two colonels. "Colonel Livingston, you get through to Polk and Hardee, Colonel Virden, you see Bragg and Breckinridge. Tell them to reestablish the integrity of their divisions, then continue in a coordinated attack."

"Very good sir," both colonels replied, saluting.

Beauregard turned to Abner. "Very well, Lieutenant, you may tell General Johnston that I am complying with his order."

"Yes, sir," Abner said saluting, then remounting for the ride back.

When Abner returned from his mission, he saw General Johnston heading toward a peach orchard that was occupied by several pieces of Confederate artillery. The trees were in full bloom, and each time one of the guns would fire, the concussion would cause the flower petals to come fluttering down in a bright pink blizzard.

Across the way from the peach orchard a little band of Yankees stubbornly held onto a piece of elevated ground. Twice they had repelled the charges made by the Bexar Fusiliers. On the second charge, Colonel Culpepper and two of his officers were killed, and now the Texans were milling around, as if wondering what to do next.

"Come on, boys!" Johnston shouted to the Texans. "We must dislodge them from that position! Do it for your fallen commander! I will lead you!"

Holding a tin coffee cup he had just liberated as if it were a saber, Johnston rode at a gallop toward the Yankee defenders. With a Rebel yell, the men in gray surged after him. This time the Yankees gave way, and the small hill was captured. Johnston came riding back, smiling broadly, his uniform torn and one boot-sole shot away.

"They didn't trip us up that time," he said. "We carried the day, boys. We carried the day. Tonight, we will water our horses in the Tennessee river."

Suddenly Johnston began reeling in his saddle.

Ralph Compton

"General, are you hurt?" Abner asked.

"Yes, and I fear seriously," Johnston replied quietly. He put his hand to his forehead.

Abner jumped down from his horse and moved quickly to help the general out of his saddle. Johnston, who had now grown very weak and pale, lay down under a tree. Isham Harris, the governor of Tennessee, saw Johnston down and he came over quickly to see what was wrong.

"Where are you hurt, General?" Harris asked.

"I . . . I truly don't know," Johnston answered. "But I have suddenly become very . . . dizzy."

Harris started unbuttoning Johnston's clothes, looking for the wound. Then he found it, a small, clean hole just above the hollow of the knee. From that neat bullet hole, Johnston was pumping blood profusely, the result of a cut artery. Harris put his hand over the wound, trying to stop the flow, but he was unable to do so.

"General, you seem to be bleeding very badly, and I don't know how to stop it. Tell me what I should do."

Johnston's eyelids fluttered, and he tried to talk, but he no longer had the strength to speak.

"Maybe some brandy," Harris suggested. From his hip pocket he took a flask, then he tried to pour some liquor into the wounded man's mouth, but the brandy just rolled right back out again, unswallowed.

"Try to take some down, General. Please try to take some down."

"Sir, apply a tourniquet," Abner suggested.

"A tourniquet?" Harris replied, obviously confused by the term. He shrugged. "I don't know what a tourniquet is."

Quickly, Abner removed his belt and wrapped it around the general's leg, just above the wound. Putting a stick in it, he twisted it down as tightly as he could get it, then he looked into Johnston's face.

"General! General! Can you hear me?" Abner shouted.

When there was no answer, Abner lifted Johnston's eyelid with his thumb and looked into his eye, then leaned forward to listen to Johnston's chest. Finally, with a sigh, he took off the impromptu tourniquet and stood up.

"Is he . . . ?" Governor Harris asked.

"Dead," Abner replied, answering the unfinished question. He started toward his horse.

"Where are you going?" Harris asked.

Abner mounted. "General Beauregard must be told," Abner said.

"What are your orders, General?" Abner asked after informing Beauregard that Johnston was dead.

"You are relieved of your duties as an aide-de-camp," Beauregard said. "You may return to your own regiment."

"Thank you, sir."

"As soon as you return, inform Colonel Culpepper."

"Colonel Culpepper is dead, sir."

"Very well, inform whoever is in command that we will continue our attacks against the Sunken Road. The Yankees are holding there and we must dislodge them."

"General, we have already launched twelve separate attacks against that road, all without success," said a colonel with a smoke-blackened face. "And the toll has been terrible," he added. "Each time we make an attack, we must climb over the bodies of the men who were killed previously."

"Then we will launch attack number thirteen," Beuregard insisted. "And this one will not fail. I have ordered artillery support."

Abner watched as the heavy guns were brought up from other places on the field. One by one the caissons were unlimbered, swung around, then anchored in place. The gun crews went about their business of loading the guns with powder, grape, and canister. Then, at nearly point-blank range, sixty-two guns opened up on the defenders in the Sunken Road. The Hornet's Nest, as both armies were now calling this place, was enveloped in one huge crashing explosion of grapeshot, shrapnel, shards of shattered rock, and splintered trees.

Finally, the artillery barrage stilled and the Confederates launched their attack, not running and screaming across the field, but marching as if on parade. Abner Murback, who, only two days earlier had been a private, was now commanding one of the companies of the Fusiliers, and he marched in front of his men, his pistol drawn.

For a moment it was quiet, except for the beating of the drums, the jangle of equipment, and the brush of footsteps. It was so quiet that Abner could hear talking in the Yankee lines.

"Here come the Rebs," someone said.

"My God, ain't they ever goin' to quit? We done kilt near as many people as they got in the whole state of Mississippi."

The Confederates continued their advance. There were no challenging Rebel yells, no cheers, no vitality in their movements. Scattered throughout the first rank were the drums, whose cadence not only kept the men marching as one but relayed the officers' orders as well. The drummers were young, some as young as twelve, but already their eyes were glazed over with the same hollow stare as those of their older comrades.

Abner led his men down to the creek, then into it. The backwater slough was knee-deep with mud and stagnant standing water, and it slowed the attackers' advance even more.

"Fire!" the Yankee artillery commander shouted.

In one horrendous volley, more than sixty cannon fired, belching out flame, smoke, and whistling death. The artillery barrage was followed almost immediately by a volley of deadly accurate riflefire. Hundreds of attacking soldiers went down in the withering fire, and the attack was stopped in its tracks. The remaining Confederate soldiers turned and scrambled back out of the water, up the embankment, and into the timberline beyond, leaving their dead and dying behind them.

One of the dead left on the field was Lieutenant Abner Murback of Bexar County, Texas.

Chapter Seven

"Oh, James, no," James's mother, Alice, said when he told her of his plans. "I have been so thankful that you didn't leave with the regiment, so happy that you were going to be here with us. Now you say you want to go off to who knows where and hunt for gold? What about your leg? The doctor told me himself how lucky you were that you didn't lose that whole leg when you were shot."

"That was a long time ago, Mom," James replied. "And you know yourself, I haven't had the least bit of trouble with it since it healed. Not even so much as a twinge."

"Still, I don't know why you would want to go to what seems like half way around the world, just to look for gold. Especially when there is no guarantee that you will even find any. Just answer me why?"

"Why? Mom, do you have any idea how

many fortunes were made during the California gold rush?"

"What do you need a fortune for? We have the ranch, and it's doing very well," his mother said.

"It's not just the money," James replied.

"Well, if it isn't the money, what is it?"

"It's, well, I don't know, I can't put it into words, but—"

"I think I can put it into words," James's father suggested.

"Well, if you can, Garrison Cason, I wish you would explain it," Alice said. She shook her head. "Because it is certainly beyond me."

"That's because you don't have the blood of a young man coursing through your veins. It was a hard thing James had to do, watching all the young men of the county ride off to go to war and not join them himself, to risk their danger, to share their glory," Garrison said. "A young man has a natural desire for adventure, and there is nothing more adventurous than a war."

"My Lord, Garrison, are you saying he should have gone to war?"

"No, I'm not saying that. Certainly, not to this war, anyway. I'm just saying that I can understand his need for adventure. And it just may be that going off to look for gold might satisfy that need."

"So, you think he should go?"

"If he wants to, yes," Garrison said. "After all, he's a man, fully grown. There's nothing we could do to stop him, anyway. Think of it, Alice. Isn't this better than going to war?"

Alice sighed in resignation. "Yes, I suppose it is," she admitted.

"I'm glad you can see it that way, Dad. And, Mom, I hope you understand," James said.

"Who is going with you?" Garrison asked.

"Well, Bob's going. Also, Billy Swan, and Duke Faglier."

"Bob's a good man, of course. And so is Billy Swan," Garrison said. "But . . . Duke Faglier? I don't know anything about him. He's the fella that works at the livery, isn't he?"

"Yes, sir."

"I don't know as I've ever said three words to him."

"He's the quiet type, all right. And unlike a lot of fellas his age, he doesn't talk about himself much. But I've known him for nearly half a year now, and he's a decent sort. He manages to avoid trouble."

"Afraid of a fight?" Garrison asked.

James chuckled. "More like fights are afraid of him."

"What do you mean?"

"It's a funny thing, I don't know if I can explain it, but on the few times he's come close to a fight, the other party has sort of backed away at the last minute. It's like they sense something about him."

"Oh, honey, you make him sound dangerous," his mother said.

"I guess he is dangerous to anyone who is his enemy. But he's proven to be just as loyal to those who call themselves his friends."

"Tell me, James, do you think this Faglier could work with cattle?"

"To tell the truth, Dad, Duke strikes me as being someone who could pretty much do anything he set his mind to. Why do you ask?"

"I've had a thought," Garrison said.

"You aren't going to try and talk me out of going to Dakota, are you? Because I am going."

"No, I'm not going to try and change your mind. On the contrary, I want you to go. But I have an idea that I believe would make the trip very profitable, even if you didn't find gold. It would be hard work, and dangerous, even more dangerous than just going after gold."

"Well, for heaven's sake, Garrison, if it is more dangerous, why are you even suggesting it?" Alice asked.

"Because nothing worthwhile can be obtained without some risk," Garrison replied.

"What is your idea?" James asked.

"I would like for you to drive some cattle up to Idaho," Garrison said. "Even though you say this won't be as big a gold rush as happened in California, there will be a lot of people there. A gold find has a tendency to draw them. And if there are a lot of people, there will be a demand for a lot of food. Those folks are going to have a real hunger for beef, and my bet is, they'll be willing to pay top dollar for cattle."

James smiled, and slapped his hand against the top of the table. "Dad, that is a great idea!" he said. "Yes, I'll do it."

"Of course, with Billy going, his Uncle Loomis will be wanting to send some of their cattle up as well. And Dusty Ferguson has been running his own cattle in with mine for many years now, so I reckon Bob will be taking some of the Ferguson cows up as well."

"Garrison, you aren't expecting four boys to take a herd all the way to Dakota by themselves, are you?" Alice asked.

"Well, to begin with, Alice, they aren't boys, they are men. But no, I don't expect them to do it by themselves. I'm sure if they look around, they'll be able to find some more folks to go with them. Hell, I'm tempted to go with them myself."

Alice shook her head vigorously. "Garrison Cason, don't you even think such a thing," she said.

Garrison laughed. "Well, I'm not going with them, Alice, but that doesn't mean I'm not going to think about it. It's going to be quite an adventure, and I like adventure as much as the next fella. I would not have come to Texas in the first place, if I didn't have a taste for adventure."

"Yes, and look where that taste for adventure almost got you. You were headed for the Alamo, intent on joining up with Travis and the others. If you had gotten there in time, we wouldn't even be having this conversation now," Alice said.

"That's all ancient history," Garrison said. "All I'm saying is, if I didn't have a ranch to run, and you to look after, I'd be on this drive with them."

"You'd be welcome to come along, Dad," James said.

Garrison laughed. "I'm sure you young people wouldn't want an old geezer like me. Don't worry, I've no intention of coming."

"Well, I would hope not," Alice said, her voice reflecting her relief.

"You want to take a herd of cattle all the way to Dakota?" Duke Faglier asked when James told him what they had planned.

"I'm taking a thousand head," James said. "Billy is taking a thousand head for his uncle. And Bob is taking five hundred head. What do you say?"

"Well, I don't know," Duke hesitated. "Driving a herd of cattle up to Dakota seems a mite more involved than just ridin' up to look for gold."

James smiled. "I can understand that—if you have no vested interest. But see if this won't change your opinion of the operation. I've talked Pa into givin' you a hundred head of your own. Mr. Swan said he'd throw in another hundred head, and Bob's pa is willin' to give you fifty. That way you'd have your own stake in this drive."

Duke was surprised by the offer. "You folks would do that?" he asked.

"Yes."

"Well, I don't know what to say. That's awful generous of you fellas."

"Trust me, Duke, you are going to earn it," Bob replied. "I know you are from Missouri and haven't really been around cows all that much, but there ain't nothin' harder'n makin' those ornery bastards move when they don't want to."

The others laughed at Bob's description.

"He said that right," Billy said. "You find a place that's hotter'n hell in the summer, colder'n the North Pole in the winter, drier than the desert sometimes, and wetter'n the ocean other times and, like as not, there will be some cows there."

Duke laughed. "Now it sounds like you boys are trying to talk me out of it."

"Not at all," James said. "We just want you to know what you're getting into, that's all."

Duke nodded. "Well, if you folks are serious about all this, count me in," he said. "Well, 250 head, huh? What do you reckon they'll bring up in Dakota?"

"I'd be willin' to bet they'll bring fifty dollars a head," Billy said.

"Fifty dollars a head? Times two-hundred-fifty? Why, that's"—he thought for a moment—"that's twelve thousand, five-hundred dollars! That's a fortune!"

"My, my, that Missouri boy can do his numbers," Bob teased, and the others laughed.

"Imagine that," Duke said, smiling broadly. "Who would've ever thought Duke Faglier would be a man of substance?"

"How soon do you reckon we can get started?" Billy asked.

"Well, since Bob's pa is foreman at Long Shadow, his beeves are already there. And that means that a hundred fifty of Duke's cows are there as well, so why don't you bring your herd on over? We'll get 'em all together before we start the drive."

"We'll help you bring 'em over," Bob offered.

"Yeah, me, too," Duke said. "I might as well get used to being around those creatures."

"Ha, what you mean is, you want to make

certain you get your one hundred head brought over," Billy said.

Duke laughed with the others.

The sign outside Bowman's Mercantile advertised DEALING IN QUALITY GOODS FOR ALL MANKIND, and Ira Bowman made an honest effort to live up to that claim. His sprawling store sold goods that spanned the spectrum from baby beds to caskets. In between were such things as harness and saddles, furniture, and ready-made clothing.

Revelation Scattergood, a young woman of twenty, was looking at a table that was piled high with men's trousers. She took one of the smaller pairs of pants from the table, then held them against her lithe form to check the fit. Deciding it was a fit, she put the pants with two others she had already laid aside.

The little bell over the door tinkled as Meg Murback and her mother came in. Without so much as a glance toward Revelation, the two women went toward the "ready to wear" dress rack.

"Oh, Mama, look at this one," Meg said, pulling out a pink dress to show. "Isn't it pretty?"

"Good afternoon, Miss Murback, Mrs. Murback, I'll be right with you," Bowman said from the back of the store.

"Did the new hats come in, Mr. Bowman?" Meg asked.

"They did indeed, direct from New Orleans. I hope you find one you like. What with the war and all, we probably won't be getting any more for a while," Bowman said.

Revelation watched as Meg picked one of the hats up and put it on. Meg walked over to the mirror and examined herself. When she saw Revelation's reflection in the mirror, looking at her, she turned toward Revelation. "And just what are *you* looking at?" she asked, contemptuously.

Revelation looked away quickly.

"Meg!" Mrs. Murback scolded. "Be quiet."

Revelation felt a small sense of consolation that Meg's mother had called her down for such a curt remark. But her satisfaction was short-lived because of what Mrs. Murback said next.

"You know better than to talk to the likes of her. Any woman who would wear men's trousers is nothing but trash."

Turning toward Revelation, Meg stuck her tongue out, then hurried away quickly to join her mother, who was examining the latest shipment of ribbons.

With her cheeks flaming in embarrassment and suppressed anger, Revelation held up the three pair of trousers.

"Put these on my bill, will you, Mr. Bowman?"

"Be glad to," Bowman answered.

Both Murback women were quiet until Revelation left the store, then Mrs. Murback spoke up.

"Ira, for the life of me, I don't know how you can stand to do business with trash like the Scattergoods," she said.

"They are good customers," Bowman replied. "They've never given me a moment's trouble and they've always paid their bills on time."

"They're cattle thieves," Mrs. Murback said.

"Nobody has ever proven that."

"Nobody has to prove it. Everyone knows it. Besides, none of the Scattergoods went to war."

"We have several who didn't go to war," Bowman reminded them. "Including James Cason." He looked pointedly at Meg.

"I have informed Mr. Cason that I want nothing to do with a man who would not do his duty," Meg said.

"Well, if you ask me, they are all slackers. But the Scattergoods are the worst of the lot," Mrs. Murback said. "If, God forbid, my son Abner doesn't come back, it's going to be awfully hard to see healthy young men walking around without a scratch on them."

"Still, you can't hold it against Revelation because her brothers didn't go off to fight in the war," Bowman suggested.

"I don't know why I can't. She is clearly the worst of the lot, and I've no doubt whatsoever that she wouldn't have gone if she had been a man. I just don't see how you can do business with them."

"I don't have to like everyone I do business with," Bowman said. "But as long as I do business with the public, seems to me like I have an obligation to serve everyone."

Revelation Scattergood was one of five children. She was twenty years old, her brothers Matthew and Mark were twenty-three and twenty-two respectively. Luke and John, the twins, were twenty-one. Revelation's mother died when Revelation was only newborn, leaving Ebeneezer Scattergood to raise his brood alone.

"He didn't raise them," someone once said, when another had commented on how difficult it must've been for Ebeneezer to raise five children on his own. "Hell, he just let them young'uns grow up like weeds. They're just as tough and just as mean as weeds, too. And the girl? She ain't a bit different; she's as tough as any of her brothers."

"Who can blame her? I reckon if you lived with a bunch like that, you'd probably try and survive any way you could."

*　　*　　*

After Revelation left Bowman's Mercantile, she stopped at the shoe store where she bought a pair of boots, then at the apothecary to pick up a nostrum for Luke's toothache. It wasn't until she returned to the livery where she had left the buckboard that she heard the liveryman, Michael Thornton, talking with Ian McMurtry about the upcoming cattle drive to Dakota.

"The four of 'em is takin' a herd of near three thousand cows all the way to Dakota, is what I hear," Thornton said.

"Sure now, an' who would be so crazy as to do such a thing?" McMurtry asked. McMurtry was in the freighting business, and he owned half a dozen freight wagons that he kept parked at the livery.

"James Cason is the one puttin' it together, I understand. And of course, whenever you see James, you gotta figure Bob Ferguson is goin' to be with 'im. Them two boys been friends since they was just just little fellas, what with Dusty Ferguson bein' Garrison Ferguson's foreman all these years. Billy Swan, and Duke Faglier is the other two."

"Duke Faglier, you say. And would that be the lad that works for you?"

"He did work for me. He give me his notice last Friday."

"He's a good worker, that lad."

"Very good, very dependable," Thornton said. "And quiet, too, the kind of quiet that makes a body wonder just what is goin' on in that head of his. But he never was any trouble. I'm goin' to hate losin' him."

"Sure an' they must be payin' him pretty good for him to give up steady work."

"He told me he was getting two hundred fifty head give to him as his share."

"Did he now? Two hundred and fifty cows you say?" McMurtry said. "Aye, that would be enough to turn the head of any ambitious lad."

"Duke said they told him cows is bringin' fifty dollars a head up in Dakota," Thornton said.

McMurtry whistled. "Fifty dollars a head? My, 'tis a king's ransom, that is. But if you ask me, they'll not get the job done. They've more'n a thousand miles to go, and it'll take 'em a good three months, even if they can keep the herd together, which I don't think they can. 'Tis more of a task than four wee lads can handle, I'm thinkin'."

Thornton looked around then and was startled to see Revelation standing there.

"My word, Revelation, why didn't you say something? Here I was just gabbing away, and you're here for your buckboard."

"That's all right, Mr. Thornton," Revelation said. "I'm in no particular hurry. What do I owe you?"

"Well, your team has been fed and watered. Twenty-five cents ought to do it. You want me to bring it around for you?"

"No, I'll get it, thank you," Revelation said, handing him a quarter from her coin purse.

Thornton and McMurtry watched Revelation as she strolled across the wagon yard toward her team and buckboard.

"You know, with her fair hair and green eyes, she could be a colleen from the old sod, that's for sure. And 'tis a fair lass she might well be, if only she would dress like one," McMurtry said.

"Perhaps, but that's not anything we're going to ever see," he said.

"Too bad. If the poor lass looked a wee bit more like a woman, I'm thinkin' she could get herself a husband. I'm believing the women would be a mite easier on her if she had a man of her own."

Thornton laughed. "Anyone who would marry her would have to tame her first, and I don't think the man has been born who can do that. Did you see what she did to Cleetus Monroe that time?"

"Sure, Michael, an' aren't you for rememberin' that I was standin' right by your side when it happened?"

McMurtry's declaration that he had witnessed it did not deter Thornton from telling what he considered to be a good story.

"Ol' Cleetus got it in his mind that he was goin' to take her britches off, to see if she really was a woman under there," Thornton began. "But she got away from him, then grabbed a whip and pret' near cut him to ribbons. He was on the ground, all covered up, cryin' and beggin' for mercy before she stopped."

"Aye, and prayin' to the Mother of our Lord to save him, and him not even being Catholic," McMurtry concluded, laughing with Thornton as they recalled the event.

To Thornton's surprise, Revelation came walking back toward them. At first he was concerned that she may have overheard them talking, and he wondered if she were going to make a scene. He was relieved when she seemed to be totally unaware that they had been talking about her.

"Mr. McMurtry, do you still have that wagon for sale?"

"Aye," McMurtry said. "A sturdy Studebaker wagon it is, as fine a wagon as you'll find in these parts, I'm thinkin'."

"And you have the mules to pull them?"

"Aye, lass, that I do. 'Tis a good strong team they are."

"Is it right that there are no other wagons or mules to be had anywhere else?"

"That's right," McMurtry said. "The army of the Confederacy bought up all the rest of the stock, rolling and live. My wagon and team is all that's left."

"How much do want for the wagon and team?"

"Five hundred dollars for the wagon, three hundred dollars for a matched team. It'll cost you eight hundred dollars, all together."

"That's a lot of money."

"Aye, it's a wee steep, but 'tis a good wagon and a good team. There's folks payin' that much for any kind of wagon and team, sure an' they are that dear now."

"All right, you hitch up the team. I'll go to the bank and get a draft for eight hundred dollars."

"Forgive me, lass, for being a bit o' the skeptic," McMurtry said. "But will the bank be for honoring your draft?"

Thornton cleared his throat. "I'll speak up for the girl," he said. "She handles all the business for the family."

"Why is that now? Herself being a woman?" McMurtry asked.

"Because the truth is, her brothers are so downright ornery that nobody wants to have anything to do with them," Thornton answered. He touched the brim of his hat. "Forgive me, Revelation, for speakin' ill of your kin."

"When it's the truth, there's no need to apologize," Revelation said. "Mr. Thornton, if you don't mind, I'll just leave the buckboard here for a while longer. Either I or one of my brothers will call for it later."

"That'll be fine," Thornton said.

"I'll be right back with your money," Revelation said to McMurtry.

Both men watched as the young woman walked toward the bank. Then Thornton turned to McMurtry. "Well, don't just stand there, man. Get the team hitched up."

Long Shadow Ranch:

After Billy Swan put his cows in with the traveling herd, all four boys bunked at Long Shadow while making preparations to leave. This worked no hardship on the ranch, as the bunkhouse was empty, that condition having come about when, to a man, all the hands left with the Bexar Fusiliers. Bob Ferguson's mother had been cooking for the ranch for many years, so it was an easy thing for her to cook for the young men.

James Cason slept and ate in the bunkhouse as well, though his mother would have preferred that he continue to live in the main house.

"After all, you are going to be gone a long time," she argued.

But Garrison defended James's choice to sleep in the bunkhouse, reminding his wife that her son would be living very closely with the young men for all the time they were gone, and it was a good thing that they start getting used to doing everything together now.

"Then perhaps I'll just clean the place up for them. I'm sure the cowboys left it a mess."

"Alice Cason, you'll do no such thing," Garrison said. "There are some places that are a man's domain, and the bunkhouse is one of those places."

"Betty Ferguson goes in the bunkhouse all the time," Alice protested.

"That's different. Mrs. Ferguson cooks for the outfit, and she always has."

"May I remind you that there is no outfit anymore?" Alice said. "Your cowboys have all gone to war, every single one, leaving you high and dry."

"That's where you are wrong, Alice. We have a fine company of young men now." Garrison looked pensive for a moment. "I just hope they are able to persuade a few others to go with them."

Mrs. Ferguson was already serving supper when Duke Faglier came in. He took his hat off, hung it on a peg, then washed his face and hands at the basin.

"Sorry I'm late, Mrs. Ferguson," Duke said as he dried his hands.

"That's quite all right, Duke. The food is still warm."

"Any luck?" James asked, passing the mashed potatoes to Duke as he sat down. The others looked toward Duke as he answered.

Spooning the mashed potatoes onto his plate, Duke shook his head slowly. "None. There's nobody left in the entire county who is willing to ride for forty and found. Especially if they have to wait until the cattle are delivered before they are paid."

"I'm not surprised," Dusty Ferguson said.

"Why's that, Pop?" Bob asked. "Forty and found seems a reasonable enough wage."

"Oh, it was at one time. But now most of the young men have gone off to war. Those who are left are at a premium, and they know it."

"What are we going to do, James? I don't think the four of us can handle a herd this large."

James sighed. "I guess about the only thing we can do is cut back on the size of the herd."

"Cut back how much?" Billy asked.

"I'd say by half."

Duke chuckled.

"What is it?" Billy asked. "What's so funny?"

"Now I know what it's like to be a big rancher," Duke said. "I've just lost half my herd, and I haven't even started yet."

The others laughed with him.

"If that is all that befalls you during this adventure, you'll consider yourselves lucky enough," Dusty said.

Chapter Eight

"The herd is gathered," Billy Swan said to James, as he swung down from his horse. "Bob and Duke are watching them now."

"Good," James answered, almost offhandedly. He had his hands on his hips and was looking at the three wagons he had lined up in front of him. He shook his head slowly.

"What's the problem?" Billy asked.

"I thought sure we would be able to get at least one good wagon out of these three," James replied. He pointed to them. "But even if I took parts off one to fix the other, I don't think I could come up with a wagon that would make the trip. Like as not it would break down about halfway there, then we would be in worse shape than when we started."

"Well, these are just little trap wagons, anyway," Billy said, taking them in with a wave of his hand. "They aren't really designed for a long trip."

"I guess I'll ride into town to see what I can find," James said, starting toward his horse. "We can't make the trip without a wagon."

" 'Tis sorry I am to be tellin' you this, lad," McMurtry said after James inquired about the purchase of a wagon. "But sure'n I sold my last wagon and team to the Scattergoods."

"The Scattergoods?" James said. "You sold the last wagon in Bexar County to the Scattergoods?"

"To the lass, actually," McMurtry said. "Revelation bought the wagon and the team."

"Why would you sell to people like that?" James asked.

"There's really no big mystery as to why, lad. I had a wagon for sale, and the lass offered the askin' price. 'Tis not for you to be tellin' me now who I can and who I can't sell to."

In frustration, James ran his hand through his hair. "You're right," he said. "But I still need a wagon. Are you sure you don't have a wagon you can sell?"

"The only wagons I have left I'm usin' for the freight line," McMurtry said. "I've none to spare."

"Do you know where a wagon can be had?"

McMurtry shook his head. "Sorry, lad, I don't."

*   *   *

It was late afternoon by the time James returned to Long Shadow. The others were already sitting at the supper table when he arrived. All of them looked toward him, the unasked question on their faces.

"No wagons to be found—anywhere," James said, disgustedly.

"When I was working at the stable, Mr. McMurtry told me he had a wagon for sale," Duke said. "What happened to it?"

James forked a pork chop onto his plate before he answered. "He sold it to Revelation Scattergood," James said glumly.

The Scattergood Spread:

"Would you mind tellin' me just what the hell we need with a wagon like that?" Matthew Scattergood asked his sister.

"It's the last wagon of its kind within a hundred miles of here," Revelation explained.

"So?" Matthew asked.

"Wait a minute, Matthew, I think I'm beginnin' to see what Revelation is talkin' about," Mark said. "If this here is the last wagon of its kind, and we own it, why, I reckon we can sell it for just about anything we want to ask for it."

"Yeah," Luke said. "And I know who we can sell it to."

"Who?" John asked.

"We can sell it to ol' James Cason and his bunch. I hear they are tryin' to hire enough drovers at forty dollars a month and found to take a herd of cattle up to Dakota. They ain't havin' much luck gettin' anyone to ride with them, but if they manage to put an outfit together, they're goin' to be needin' a sturdy wagon and a good team of mules."

"Ha, that's right!" Mark said. He laughed. "And anyone stupid enough to try and push cows all the way to Dakota is prob'ly stupid enough to pay twice what this wagon is worth." He looked at Revelation. "I don't care what the others say about you, Sis, I think what you done was real smart. Yes, sir, we'll turn a pretty penny on this wagon."

"We aren't going to sell it," Revelation replied.

"What? What do you mean we ain't goin' to sell it?" Mark asked. "What the hell are we goin' to do with it if we don't sell it?"

"We're going to take it to Dakota. Along with five hundred head of cows. We're going to join the Cason outfit."

"What?" Matthew exploded. "Now you've done it! I always know'd you was a little touched, but this time you have gone over the edge. Whatever got it in your mind that we would drive five hundred head of cows all the way to Dakota?"

"Yeah, have you gone completely crazy?" Luke added.

John pointed to his temple and made a circling motion with his finger. The others laughed.

"When we sell our cattle here, how much do we get for them?" Revelation asked.

"Maybe ten, fifteen dollars a head," Mark answered. He laughed. "We can't be none too particular about the price since we ain't always that particular about what brand our cow is wearin'."

The others laughed.

"Exactly," Revelation replied. "What if I told you that we could get fifty dollars a head for our cattle in Dakota?" Revelation asked.

"Why would anyone pay that much for a cow?" John asked.

"Wait a minute," Mark said. "Revelation might be on to somethin'. I hear tell there's a gold rush goin' on up there now. I been thinkin' about maybe goin' up there to look for some gold myself. But my guess is, there are probably some hungry folks up there about now. I 'spect a little beef would taste real good to 'em."

"Fifty dollars a head? How much money would that be?" Matthew asked.

"Twenty-five thousand dollars," Revelation replied. "That's five thousand dollars for each of us."

Luke whistled. "Jumpin' Jehoshafphat, that is a lot of money."

"Plus, don't forget, once we get up there we can do some of our lookin' for gold," Mark suggested.

"You know what I'm thinkin'?" Matthew asked. "I'm thinkin' them boys up there is prob'ly about as thirsty as they are hungry."

"You're sayin' we should take some of our whiskey?" Mark asked.

"And our whiskey distillery," Matthew said. He smiled broadly. "You know, this goin' to Dakota may turn out to be about the best idea I've ever had."

"You always have had a good head for business, Matthew," Revelation said. She didn't care who got credit for the idea of going to Dakota. The only thing she cared about was that they go. Matthew was the oldest, and now that he was committed to it, the battle was won. They would be going. Assuming, of course, that Cason and the others let them go.

Billy was the first one to see the wagon coming up the long road that led out to the ranch from El Camino Real, the pike that ran into town. He pointed it out to the others.

"Who do you suppose it is?" Billy asked.

"I don't know who it is," Duke replied. "But I know what it is. That's the wagon McMurtry had for sale. I recognize it."

"Then, no doubt, one of the Scattergoods is

driving it," James said. "Probably coming out here to sell the wagon to us."

"Yeah, and for twice what they paid for it, I'm bettin'," Bob said.

"If so, there's nothing we can do about it," Billy said. "We need the wagon. We'll have to pay whatever they are asking."

"Maybe not," James suggested. "I mean, sure it would be nice to have a wagon, but we're already planning to use pack animals, and if we have to we will. On the other hand, if they can't sell that wagon to us, what can they do with it? Looks to me like this is about a standoff. And if we handle it right, we might wind up getting a pretty good bargain after all."

"I wonder which one of them it is?" Bob asked.

"As far as I'm concerned, it doesn't make any difference which one it is," Billy replied. "There ain't a one of 'em worth the powder it would take to blow them apart."

"Well, let's go talk to him," James suggested, starting toward his horse. "We may have a little surprise for him when he starts dealing."

The surprises went the other way. The first surprise was when they realized that it wasn't one of the Scattergood men they would be dealing with but their sister, Revelation. The second surprise was when she told them the wagon wasn't for sale.

"Not for sale?" James sputtered. "Well, if the wagon isn't for sale, I don't understand. Why did you bring it out here?"

"I wanted you to see it," Revelation replied. "I want you to realize what a great wagon it would make for your drive to Dakota."

"Uh-huh," James said. "So you're just trying to goad us, is that it?"

Revelation smiled and when she did, an amazing transformation took place. Although dressed as a man, in trousers, denim shirt, and a decrepit old felt hat, the smile lit up her face. Her eyes flashed, her dimples deepened, and it was quite easy to see that she was a woman.

"No, Mr. Cason, I don't want to goad you," she said. "I want to join you."

"Join us?"

"I want to go to Dakota with you."

James laughed.

"Do you find the idea of my going to Dakota funny?"

"Yes," James answered.

"I'm told that you've not been able to hire anyone to go with you."

"Don't need anyone," James replied. "We're going to make the drive ourselves."

"Four of you are going to drive nearly three thousand cattle over a thousand miles? And with no wagon?" she added.

"Maybe our herd won't be quite as large as all that," James said.

Revelation nodded. "I don't blame you. With no drovers to move the cows, and no wagon, then the smaller you keep your herd, the better it will be for you. Of course, the payoff at the other end won't be nearly as large."

"Better that we get there with a few, than that we leave cows stranded over the eighteen hundred miles between here and there."

"Perhaps. But it would be better still if you got there with all the cattle you originally planned to take."

"And you think your going with us can accomplish that?" James asked.

"Me . . ." Revelation replied. She nodded at the wagon and team. "My wagon and team . . ." She paused for a moment longer before continuing. "And my four brothers."

"Your four brothers?"

"You'd have plenty of drovers to help you with the herd if they came," Revelation added.

Billy snorted. "Ha! I can't see your brothers working for forty and found."

Revelation shook her head. "Oh no, we wouldn't work for anything like that."

James's face reflected a look of confusion. "Then I don't understand. If you won't work for forty and found, what will you work for? What do you want?"

"We want nothing," Revelation said. "Except the right to throw our herd in with yours during the drive."

"Your herd?"

"A thousand head. For that, you have five more hands—"

"Five?"

"Counting me," Revelation said. "I can work as hard as any man."

James shook his head. "A thousand head? No. Even with four more—five more hands," he corrected himself, "a thousand more head would make the herd too large to handle."

"What about seven hundred fifty head?" Revelation proposed.

"Make it five hundred and we have a deal," James countered.

"Done," said Revelation.

"James, you think that's wise?" Billy asked, surprised that James had accepted Revelation's offer.

"Think about it," James said. "With five more hands and a wagon, we can take our entire herd."

"I agree with James," Bob said. "What about you, Duke?"

Duke demurred. "I'm not sure I rightly have a voice in this," he said.

"Sure you do. You've got your own herd, same as the rest of us."

"Well, if the difference is between taking all our cows or paring down because we have to travel light-handed, then I'm for adding the extra hands."

"All right," Billy said. "If you fellas are willing to take a chance on them, I reckon I am, too."

"Go get your brothers," James said. "Come back with them and the wagon, ready to go."

"Give me the loan of a horse," Revelation said, "and I'll leave the wagon here so you can get started loading."

"All right," James said. "Oh, there's one more thing. Since you and your brothers are partners, rather than riding for forty and found, you'll be expected to come up with your share of money for the drive."

"Fair enough," Revelation said. "We'll bring the money with us when we return."

"How do we know we can trust you to have the money?" Bob asked.

"Simple. If we don't have the money, we don't go. If we do have the money, we do go."

"Sounds reasonable enough to me," Billy said.

"What about the cattle?" James asked.

"What about them?" Revelation replied.

"Word is you Scattergoods aren't always that particular about whose brand is on the cows you run. I wouldn't want to get jumped by a posse somewhere, claiming we're driving stolen cattle."

"There will be no posse," Revelation assured them.

"If anyone does prove you are running their cattle, you and your brothers will have to leave."

"That's fair enough."

"Without your cows," James added.

"What are you saying? That you would expect us to just leave our cows behind?"

James shook his head. "No, what I'm saying is, you better own the cows you bring to us."

Chapter Nine

Fort Worth, Texas
Wednesday, June 18, 1862:

It had taken Angus Butrum most of the morning to ride over to Fort Worth from Dallas. Dallas was a sleepy little town, but Fort Worth was full of activity, though as he looked more closely, he saw that most of the activity came from soldiers. Like ants at a picnic, the soldiers were everywhere. As far as he could tell, though, they weren't doing anything except wearing their uniforms and parading up and down the street saluting one another. Angus reined up in front of a saloon, but just before he dismounted, he worked up a good spit of tobacco and squirted it onto the boardwalk. Although he hadn't intended to do so, it got on the boots and pants of a young lieutenant. The young woman who was walking along the boardwalk with the lieutenant just managed to avoid it.

"Hey, mister, you just spit on my boots!" the lieutenant complained.

Angus looked at the officer but said nothing.

"Well, you just going to stand there like a dumb ox?" the lieutenant challenged. "Get down there and clean it off."

The girl saw the danger in Angus's eyes before the young officer did, and she pulled on his arm. "Come on, Donnie, let's go. I'll clean it."

"No," Donnie said, obviously trying to make a show of it in front of the girl. "This scoundrel is not in uniform. It is obvious that he is either too cowardly to be in the army or he is a deserter. Now, which is it, mister?"

Still silent, Angus tied his horse off at the hitching rail.

"Mister, are you mute as well as dumb? I'm talking to you."

The blood vessel in Angus's temple enlarged, then began to throb. He stared directly at the young lieutenant.

"Sonny, why don't you and your whore just pass on by?" Angus said.

"Whore?" the young woman gasped.

"I don't know where you're from, mister, but that kind of language is killing words around here. I'm calling you out!" the young officer said, his voice cracking in anger.

"No, wait, Donnie, please!" the young girl pleaded, her voice now on the verge of panic.

"It's all right. I know he was just talking. Come on, please? Let's go!"

"You better listen to the girl, sonny," Angus said.

Under normal circumstances, Donnie may have recognized the danger himself, but these weren't ordinary circumstances. Donnie was wearing the uniform of a second lieutenant in the Confederate cavalry, and carrying a new Colt pistol in his holster. Inspired with the zeal of patriotism, he was anxious to prove his manliness and bravery in front of the daughter of his commanding officer.

Donnie unsnapped the flap cover of his holster, and put his hand on the butt of his pistol.

"Now I'm going to give you one last chance. I'm going to count to three. You either apologize and clean off my boot, or go for your gun. I don't care which," Donnie said.

"Donnie, no!" the young woman said, her words now on the verge of a scream.

By now, half a dozen passersby had been drawn to the scene. When they heard Donnie's challenging words, they grew tense as they waited to see what was going to happen.

"Mandy, you get on out of the way," Donnie said, waving her away.

"Donnie, please!"

"Miss, you better get on over here," one of the onlookers said.

"What's it going to be, mister," Donnie said to Angus. "Are you going to apologize? Or do I start counting."

"Start counting," Angus said, calmly.

Donnie blinked a couple of times, then a small patina of sweat broke out across his upper lip. It was as if, until that moment, he thought he could bluff his way through. Now he realized that this man couldn't be bluffed. He also knew that he couldn't take him. But that realization had come too late. It was impossible for him to back out of it now, without spending the rest of his life in shame.

Donnie licked his lips a couple of times, then with a voice that was much less authoritative than it had been, began to count.

"One," he said. He paused, then said, "Two." Now he paused for a long time, praying that, somehow this could all go away, that this man he had challenged would apologize, or at least, turn and walk away. The man continued to look at him with a cold, unblinking stare.

"Three," Donnie said, starting his draw even as he said the word.

Angus drew and fired before Donnie could get his gun level. Donnie pulled the trigger on his own pistol very quickly behind Angus, so those who only heard the sound of the gunshots thought the fight was much closer than it really was. In truth, Donnie's bullet plunged into the boardwalk right beside him—right in the middle of the tobacco quid Angus had expectorated a few moments earlier.

"Donnie!" Mandy shouted, and pulling away from the person who tried to hold her back, she rushed to Donnie's side, looking down in his face just as he breathed his last.

"Is there anybody here who doesn't know he drew first?" Angus asked.

"Hell, mister, he was just a kid," one of the men in the quickly gathering crowd said. "You coulda walked away from it before it ever got this far."

Angus stared at the man from the crowd for a long, rather frightening moment, then he put his pistol in his holster and walked into the saloon. The saloon had been practically emptied when everyone ran outside to see what the gunshots were about. In their excitement to see what was going on, several pushed right by Angus, not realizing he had been one of the principals.

Angus saw his two brothers, Percy and Chance, standing at the bar. Though they had watched the drama unfold, they had not joined the exodus.

"What was all that about out there?" one of them asked.

"Ah, it was just some soldier-boy, too big for his britches."

"Did you have to kill 'im?"

"He didn't give me no choice. The boy wouldn't leave it alone."

"You ain't goin' to be none too popular around here," Chance said, as Angus joined them.

"Yeah, well, I got no time for some snot-nosed bastard trying to prove he's a man."

"Did you hear anything in Dallas?" Chance asked.

"No. What about you two?"

"Nobody here has ever heard of Duke Faglier."

"So, Angus, what do we do now?"

"We go on looking."

"We've been looking for that son of a bitch for a long time now," Percy said. "We come close to findin' him when he was in Springfield, but he run off before we got there."

"He deserted the army, is what he done," Chance said. "So now if we find 'im and kill 'im, we'll get us that two hundred dollar reward the blue-bellies has got for deserters."

"He wasn't in the army. He was a civilian. There ain't no reward for him," Angus said. Nearby was a half-filled mug of beer, left by a customer who had gone out with the others to see the commotion. Angus picked up the mug and began drinking.

"Maybe he's joined up with the Reb army,"

Percy suggested. "If he has, we ain't never goin' to find him."

"He didn't join up with the Rebs," Chance said.

"How do you know he didn't?"

"I just know," Angus said, reaching for still another half-filled mug.

"All right, so what do we do now?"

"We keep looking," Angus replied. "He killed two of our brothers. You boys can go on back up to Missouri if you want. But I, for one, don't intend to let him get away with that."

"I ain't desertin' you, Angus," Percy said. "Wherever you decide to go, I'll be right there with you."

"Me, too," Chance said. There was a beat of silence then he added, "Where will that be?"

"Austin first," Angus said. He drained the beer from the mug, then wiped the back of his hand across his mouth. "Then I figure maybe San Antonio."

"When do we get started?" Percy asked.

"Now," Angus said. "Right now."

Angus started toward the front door, and his two brothers were right behind him. When they reached the sidewalk, two men were gently lifting the young soldier onto the back of a buckboard.

"He's the one did it," they heard someone

say, not in an accusing tone, but almost one of awe.

Without even making eye contact with any of the townspeople who had been drawn to the macabre scene, the three brothers mounted their horses and rode south, out of town. Not one of them looked back.

Long Shadow Ranch
Wednesday, June 18, 1862:

"Looks like we're goin' to need us a couple of pack animals after all," Bob told James.

"Why is that?"

"The wagon's not big enough to hold all our stuff."

"Wait a minute," Duke said. "That can't be right. Maybe I don't know cows, but I do know wagons, and there's no reason why a big Studebaker wagon like this can't carry everything we've got to carry."

"Well, come have a look if you don't believe me," Bob invited. "I'm tellin' you, it's not going to do it."

When James and Duke rode back to the wagon with Bob, they saw several unpacked items lying around on the ground. Revelation was leaning back against the wagon with her arms folded across her chest.

"Are you sure you packed it right?" James asked, swinging down from the saddle.

"Come on, James, I've packed wagons before. See for yourself."

James looked into the wagon, then back at the items on the ground. "It looks like a good tight pack," he admitted. He shook his head. "I can't figure out why everything's not going in."

Duke looked into the wagon as well. He moved back to study the wagon from outside, then he stepped back to look down inside again.

"I'll be damned," he said.

"What is it?" James asked.

"Bob, reach underneath the wagon there," Duke said. "Put your hand on the bottom."

Bob started to do as Duke asked, but Duke redirected him. "No, do it up here," he said.

With a puzzled shake of his head, Bob walked up to the front of the wagon where Duke was standing, then he dropped to one knee and reached up from beneath the wagon to put his hand on the bottom. Duke stuck his hand down over the side of the wagon and touched the bottom from that side just above where Bob was touching. Then he looked over at Revelation.

"What are you carrying in this wagon?" Duke asked.

"I don't know what you are talking about," Revelation replied.

"The hell you don't. What are you carrying in this wagon besides vittles?"

"What is it, Duke?" James asked.

"Look how much space there is between the floor of the wagon and the bottom of the wagon. It has a false bottom."

"Glory be," James said, looking at the disparity Duke had pointed out. "You're right." He looked at Revelation. "All right, so what's going on here?" he asked. "What's under the false bottom?"

"Look, this is as much a surprise to me as it is to you. I don't know what you are talking about," Revelation insisted.

"Let's get the wagon unloaded and check it out," James said.

When Matthew and Mark Scattergood arrived on the scene a few minutes later, they saw all the supplies spread out on the ground. Duke and Bob were up in the now-empty wagon, working on the floor with a crowbar. As he pulled a nail loose, it made a terrible screeching sound.

"Here, what are you adoin' tearin' up our wagon like that?" Matthew asked, challengingly.

"We're repairing it," James explained.

"Repairing it? What do you mean, repairing it? It's purt' near new. There ain't nothin' wrong with it."

"The floor is too high," James said, innocently. "We figured if we could lower it a bit, we might be able to get all our stuff loaded."

Matthew and Mark looked at each other, their faces reflecting some concern.

"There's no need to do that. The floor's fine just the way it is," Mark said.

There was another screeching sound as a nail was removed, then the sound of a board being pulled up, followed by a shout of triumph.

"Well, now, what do we have here?" Duke asked from inside the wagon. He held up a jug.

"What is that?" James asked.

"It looks like it might be a little moonshine whiskey," Duke replied. He pulled the cork. "Smells like it, too." He turned it up and took a drink "Well now, fancy that, it *is* moonshine whiskey," Duke concluded. "Not all that good a whiskey, but whiskey, nonetheless."

"What do you mean it ain't all that good?" Mark asked in an angry spurt. "I'll have you know that's the best whiskey in the county."

"Whether it's good whiskey or bad, it has no business here," James said, pointing to the wagon.

"We thought maybe we would take some along to use for snakebite," Matthew suggested.

"Snakebite my ass," Bob said. "You were plannin' on sellin' it."

"So what if we are?" Mark responded.

"There's no law against an honest man making a living, is there?"

Bob laughed. "Honest? That's not a word you often hear in the same sentence as the name Scattergood."

Mark glared at Bob.

"How many jugs of whiskey do you have in there?" James asked.

"They're gallon jugs, we have forty-eight."

"Get it off, now."

"What will we do with it?"

"James, we don't have to get rid of all of it," Duke said. "There will be room for some. Say, eight gallons or so."

"All right," James said. "You can take eight gallons. The rest of it stays."

"You didn't answer my question," Matthew said. "What do we do with the whiskey that stays?"

"Drink it, burn it, pour it out on the ground," James said impatiently. "I don't care what you do with it. Just get it off that wagon."

There was a hollow sound as Duke pulled the cork on another jug, then a gurgling sound as he began to pour the whiskey out.

"Wait, no sense in pourin' it all out," Matthew said, climbing up onto the wagon. He picked up another jug and pulled the cork. "We may as well drink what we can."

Chapter Ten

First day of trail drive
Thursday, June 19, 1862:

When dawn broke the next morning, Matthew
and Mark Scattergood were passed out drunk.
Angrily, James ordered Luke and John to get
their brothers on their horses, even if they had
to be tied bellydown across their saddles. They
weren't tied down, but they were tied to their
saddles, their hands crossed in front of them
and secured to the saddle horn.

Everyone but Revelation had drunk a little the
night before, but no one drank as much as Matthew and Mark. In fact, James didn't think he
had ever seen anyone drink as much as they
did.

"Herd's on the move," Bob said, coming up
to him then. "Luke is riding drag, Billy and
Duke are flank and swing on the other side, I've

got John riding swing on this side and I'll ride up front as flank."

"Thanks," James said. "I'll take point."

"Say, James, have you thought of a name for our outfit yet?"

"A name?"

"Yes. We have to call it something. What shall we call it?"

"How about the Ferguson, Faglier, Swan, Scattergood, Cason Cattle Company?" James suggested.

"No, that's no good. Too long. How about the Cason Cattle Company?"

James shook his head. "No, that wouldn't be fair to everyone else. We all have a stake in the drive."

"Well, we have to call it something."

At that moment, James Cason saw a calf, hurrying quickly to catch up with its mother. The early morning sun cast a golden halo around the calf. He laughed, and pointed. "There's our name," he said.

"What?"

"Golden Calf. The Golden Calf Cattle Company."

"Yes!" Bob replied. "Yes, that's a great name."

"Think we ought to check with the others?"

"Why? I'm the one who decided we should have a name, and you are the one who came up with it. Far as I'm concerned, that's good enough."

"Then the Golden Calf Cattle Company it is,"

James said. He twisted around in his saddle. "By the way, have you seen Matthew and Mark this morning? Are they able to sit their saddle?"

"Barely. They're riding alongside the wagon."

"Will they be any use to us anytime soon? What do they look like?"

Bob chuckled. "Their eyes look like two pee holes in a snowbank," he said. "I guess they'll come around by noon. But right now the poor bastards don't have an idea of what's going on around them, except they're feeling pretty sick."

"I've never seen anyone drink that much," James said. "I thought they were taking all that whiskey to sell. I'm beginning to think now that if we had kept it, they would've drunk it all."

"I don't doubt it," Bob said.

"How are you doing?" James asked.

"What do you mean, how am I doing?"

James laughed. "I admit you didn't drink much last night, but for you, it doesn't take much. As long as I've known you, you haven't been able to hold your liquor. The smell of a cork could make you drunk. To tell the truth, I wasn't sure you'd answer the call this morning."

"Hey, you don't need to be worryin' any about me, James Cason," Bob replied. "When the tocsin sounds, I will respond."

James laughed. "You are full of it," he said. He pointed to the head of the herd. "All right, the tocsin is sounding now. Go."

Bob slapped his legs against the side of his horse and urged it into a gallop, dashing alongside the slowly moving herd until he was in the flank position, which was near the front, on the right-hand side. James rode up the side of a small hill, then looked back down on the Golden Calf Cattle Company. It made an impressive sight, over three thousand head of longhorns, five abreast and over a mile long, moving slowly but inexorably across the South Texas plain. From his position he could see the entire herd. Billy Swan was the flank rider on the left side, near the front, and Duke Faglier was on the same side, riding in the swing position, or near the rear. John was riding swing on the right and Luke was riding drag, bringing up the rear. The wagon was already a mile ahead of the herd, with Revelation sitting straight in the driver's seat. Alongside the wagon, with their horses tethered to the vehicle, the two older Scattergoods, Matthew and Mark, sat weaving in their saddles.

James had read once that any journey of a thousand miles must start with a single step. This was that step.

San Antonio, Texas
Tuesday, July 1, 1862:

It was two weeks after James and the others left San Antonio when the Butrum brothers arrived. They didn't even have to ask around to find Duke Faglier. They overheard his name when they were unsaddling their horses at the livery.

"Pardon me," Angus said to the two men who were talking. "Did I just hear you say the name Faglier?"

"My name is Thornton," the liveryman said. "I own this place."

"The name I'm interested in is Faglier. Duke Faglier," Angus said. "Didn't I just hear one of you just say that name?"

"What's it to you, mister?" Thornton asked.

"We're the Goodsons, from Missouri," Angus lied. "Duke Faglier is our cousin and we been alookin' for 'im."

Thornton smiled broadly. "Cousins, eh? Well, why didn't you say you was kin? I knew Duke was from Missouri, but that's about all I knew. Duke never talked much 'bout his past. Truth is, don't nobody around here know too much about him. But he was a good worker while he was here, and never give anybody any trouble."

"While he was here? You mean he ain't here no more?"

"Afraid not."

"What happened to him? Did he go off to fight in the war?"

"No, he didn't go off with the regiment. Him and some other fellas who didn't go are takin' a herd of cows up to Dakota."

By now, both Chance and Percy had joined their older brother, and when they heard Thornton say that Faglier was taking a herd to Dakota they looked at each other is surprise.

"Now what would he do a dumb-fool thing like that for?" Angus asked. He could barely conceal the frustration he felt at having almost found Faglier, only to miss him by a couple of weeks.

"Well, sir, that's the same question lots of us have been askin'," Thornton replied. "But when you look at it close, you see that it ain't such a dumb-fool thing after all. That is, if they can do it. They're takin' a herd of over three thousand cows up to Dakota to sell 'em to the gold miners. They figure to get fifty dollars a head for them cows."

"Gold miners? What gold miners?" Angus asked.

Thornton chuckled. "My, where have you fellas been that you ain't heard the news. They've found gold up in Dakota."

"Where?"

"According to what I've read they found it

first at a place called Grasshpopper Creek, but I reckon they're findin' it all over now. Why, from what I've heard, there are picking up nuggets as big as your thumb just clinging to the roots of the grass. Bigger, even, than the California find was, here a few years back."

"I'll be damned," Angus said.

"Will you be boardin' your horses for long?"

"What?" Angus asked, distractedly.

"Your horses," Thornton repeated. "How long will you be leaving them with me?"

"Three, four days at least," Percy said. "Maybe more."

"Uh, no," Angus said, overriding Percy's response. "We'll be takin' 'em out first thing in the mornin'."

"If you're goin' to take 'em out in the mornin', that'll be twenty-five cents apiece, in advance. If you leave 'em past noon tomorrow, it'll cost you another twenty-five cents."

"All right," Angus said. He gave Thornton the money, then started out of the livery. Percy and Chance watched him for a moment, then put their own quarters in Thornton's out-stretched hand before they hurried after him.

"What are we going to do now?" Percy asked as he and Chance caught up with Angus.

"Right now, I aim to get me a little supper, and maybe somethin' to drink," Angus said.

"I mean, in the morning," Percy said. "I

thought we was goin' to rest here for a few days."

"That was before we heard about Faglier," Angus replied.

"Listen, Angus, it ain't goin' to do none of us any good if we go out after him right away. We been ridin' hard for a long time, we need a little rest," Chance said. "Besides, if he's trailing a herd all the way up to Dakota, he ain't goin' nowhere. We can catch up with him anytime we want."

"Wait a minute," Percy said. He smiled. "Wait a minute, I know what you're doin'. I'll be damned. You're aimin' to steal them cows, aren't you?"

"No," Angus replied.

"What? Why not? Didn't you hear what that liveryman said? Them cows will be bringing fifty dollars a head up in Dakota. Why wouldn't we steal 'em?"

"Yeah," Chance said. "I'm with Percy on this, Angus. I mean, why, who knows how much money them cows would make?"

" 'Bout a hunnert and fifty thousand dollars," Angus said easily.

"A hunnert and fifty thousand dollars?" Percy gasped. "Lord, I didn't know there was that much money in the whole world."

"Wait a minute You're sayin' them cows is

worth a hunnert and fifty thousand dollars, but we ain't goin' to steal them?"

"That's what I'm sayin'."

"Damn, Angus, what's got into you? You used to be the one with all the ideas," Chance said.

Just as they reached the front of the saloon, Angus turned to his two brothers. "You want to herd those cows all the way up to Dakota? Just the three of us?"

"What are you getting at?"

Angus smiled. "I say, let them do all the work, drive the cows to Dakota, find the buyer, then sell them. That's when we'll hit them. It's going to be a lot easier to steal the money than it would be to steal the cows."

Percy laughed out loud. "Damn, that's right," he said. "So, what's the plan?"

"It's going to take them three or four months to push a herd all the way to Dakota," Percy said. "But if we ride back to Kansas City and catch a riverboat going up the Missouri, we can be there less than three weeks from now."

"So, we're going to wait on them?"

"Yes."

"Hey, Angus, while we're waiting, you think we could look for some of that gold?" Chance asked.

"Why bother to look?" Angus asked. "Why

not just take our gold off the people who have already found it?"

With the Golden Calf Cattle Company, mile 300, Friday, July 11:

Although no one had driven a herd as far as they intended to take this herd, everyone in the outfit had previous experience except Duke. Ironically, the Scattergoods had the most experience in longer drives, since they had brought most of their stock up from Mexico.

Duke's normally taciturn habit proved to be an asset to him. He talked little, listened a lot, observed, and learned. He was prepared for work, so the fact that the drive required the cowboys to be in the saddle for fifteen hours each day didn't bother him.

He found the makeup of the drive interesting. The wagon Revelation drove was the chuck wagon, which carried the food, bedding, and tents. Revelation prepared the breakfast and supper meals, and served them from the tailboard of the wagon. The food was cooked over an open fire. Lunch was generally taken in the saddle, often consisting of a cold biscuit and bacon left over from breakfast, or perhaps a piece of jerky.

The herd moved across the country, not in

one large mass, but in a long plodding column, generally no more than four or five abreast. An average day was twelve to fifteen miles, and while on the move, one of the cowboys would be riding as point man, ahead of the herd scouting for water and graze. Flankers rode on either side of the herd, keeping them moving, while one man rode drag, meaning the rear. This was the least desirable position because the cowboy who rode drag had to swallow all the dust. In many outfits, Duke, being the least experienced, would have been selected to ride drag every day. But James, who had been elected trail boss, was fair about it, and he rotated the position, even taking drag himself, when it was his turn.

Billy Swan was about five miles ahead of the herd, looking for water, when he crested a small hill and saw the military encampment. It wasn't a large group as army units were measured back East, but there were at least one hundred men there on the banks of a swiftly flowing stream. A puff of red, white, and blue hung from the top of a makeshift flagpole. However, because it was a windless day, the flag hung straight down so it was impossible to determine whether it was the Stars and Stripes of the Union, or the Stars and Bars of the Confederacy. Turning his horse around, he rode quickly back to the herd.

"Is there any way to avoid them?" James asked, when Billy reported on his find.

Billy shook his head. "I don't see how," he answered. "Not if we want to water the herd."

"We've got to water the herd," Bob said.

"And you don't know if them soldier-boys be theirs or our'n?" Mark Scattergood asked.

"Like us, you chose not to go to war," James said. "Therefore, for us, there is no theirs or ours," James said.

"What do you mean there ain't no theirs or our'n?" Mark asked. "They got to be either Yankees or Southerners."

"Listen to what I am saying. There is no theirs or ours," James repeated, saying the words slowly and distinctly. "Not if we are going to make it through over a thousand miles. All of us chose to avoid this war. That means we are neutral."

"Well, yeah, I guess we are neutral in a way," Mark said. "But we are Southerners. I mean, we do come from the South."

"We come from the West," James insisted.

"You can't just tell a fella to deny who he is," Mark insisted.

"James is right, Mark," Bob said. "That kind of thinking has no place now. We made a conscious decision to avoid the war. That means we are neutral."

"We may be neutral," Duke said. "But the men Bob saw aren't. We're going to have to come up with some way of handling them."

"I guess the best thing to do is go see them," James said. "Bob, you and Billy stay here with the herd. Duke, you come with me. You don't sound quite as Southern as the rest of us do. Maybe the two of us can convince them, whoever they are, that we aren't a threat."

As James and Bob approached the encampment, they were challenged by a sentry who suddenly popped up in front of them. He was wearing gray.

"Halt! Who goes there!" the sentry shouted, holding his rifle leveled toward them.

"The name is Cason, James Cason," James said. "We've got a herd of cows near here, that we're driving north." He nodded toward the water. "We need to bring 'em to water. If I could just talk to your commanding officer?"

Half a steer hung on a spit over an open fire, the smell of its roasting permeating the air. The soldiers were in good spirits as they contemplated the feast that lay before them. James and Major Waldron, the commanding officer of the little army unit they had encountered, were sitting on a log near the fire.

"It was very generous of you to offer up a steer like that," Major Waldron said. "My men haven't eaten anything but beans, bacon, and hardtack since we left Arkansas."

"Glad to do it," James replied. "We were having a hunger for beef ourselves, but it made no sense to kill a steer for just nine of us. It would be too much of a waste."

"How is it that you fellas aren't in the war?" Major Waldron asked.

"I've got kin on both sides," James answered.

Major Waldron got up from the log, walked over to the fire, and picked up a burning brand. Then, pulling the stub of a cigar from his pocket, he lit it, taking several long puffs. What he did next surprised James, because he pinched off the glowing end of the cigar, then returned the stub to his pocket.

"I have to ration them," he explained when he saw the surprised look on James's face. "I don't know when I'll get another one."

"I imagine that might be difficult," James said.

Major Waldron returned to the log and sat down again.

"Now, about you not wanting to fight against your kin. Well, I reckon most of us are in that same fix," the major said. "But when you get right down to it, a fella has to go with his conscience, and fight for what he believes in."

"That's the way I look at it too," James said. "And my conscience tells me—"

"You stay the hell away from her, Butler! I saw her first!"

The loud shout interrupted the conversation

between James and the army commander. When they looked toward the commotion, they saw two men in angry confrontation.

"Well, hell, Dobbins, iff'en you ain't man enough to keep her, you got no right to her," Butler replied.

"I'll show you who is man enough," Dobbins said, launching a roundhouse right at his adversary. His unexpected blow landed on Butler's chin, and though it didn't knock him down, it did drive him back a few feet.

Butler rubbed his chin, then worked his jaw back and forth a few times. When he was certain nothing had been broken, he smiled at Dobbins, an evil and mirthless smile.

"Fight, fight!" someone shouted, and the camp came alive as soldiers hurried to the scene.

The expression on Dobbins's face turned from anger to one of apprehension. He had just given Butler his best blow and Butler was able to shake it off as if it were no more than a mosquito bite.

"What the hell is going on over there?" Major Waldron asked.

Bellowing like a bull, Butler charged Dobbins. Dobbins turned and ran, chased not only by Butler, but by the laughter of the other men. That was when James saw Revelation Scattergood standing near the wagon.

He wasn't that surprised to see her, but he

was surprised to see what she was wearing. So far on this drive she had worn nothing but men's trousers and shirts. In addition, she had kept her hair pinned up under her hat.

Now, Revelation was wearing a dress, and not just any dress. She was wearing a dress that flowed with her lithe body, displaying a womanly form that the trousers had managed to hide. In addition, her hair, which James now saw was the color of ripe wheat, fell across her shoulders in soft waves. This was the first time he had ever seen her like this and he had to admit, begrudgingly, that she was an attractive woman.

"I think I see the problem," James said quietly, his voice reflecting the sense of guilt he felt over being the indirect cause.

Major Waldron also saw Revelation. "What the hell?" he asked in surprise. "Is that a camp follower? Where the hell did she come from? As far as I know there's not a town within fifty miles of here."

"She's with us," James said. "She's driving the chuck wagon."

"Hell's bells, man, don't you know better than to bring a good-looking woman like that into a camp full of soldiers?"

"I didn't realize I was," James replied.

"What do you mean? Didn't you just tell me she was driving your chuck wagon?"

"I mean I didn't know she was good-looking," James said, looking at Revelation as if he had never seen her before.

In order to prevent any further outbreaks, Major Waldron ordered his men to break camp and prepare to leave. There was a lot of grumbling from the men, and some voiced protests from the Scattergoods, who had intended to turn a fair profit on the whiskey they had remaining.

"I'm sorry if our arrival caused you any trouble," James apologized.

"It wasn't that much trouble," Major Waldron said. "Hell, men been fighting over good-looking women from the beginning of time. You can't change nature."

"No, I suppose not. Why don't you take the other half of the beef we slaughtered?"

"That's mighty big of you," Waldron said.

"We can't keep that much beef without it going bad on us," James said.

"All right, thanks, I'll get my quartermaster on it," Waldron said. He called over a big, red-haired captain, gave him the order to see to the half of beef, then came back to talk to James.

"You say you are going up to Dakota?"

"Yes."

"How are you going?"

"Just head north, I reckon."

"There's a trail I've heard about, a new trail

laid out by a fella named John Bozeman. The
Bozeman Trail. You ever heard of it?"

James shook his head. "Can't say as I have."

"It's a shortcut that will save you a lot of time.
You might want to try it."

"I will try it. Thanks for the information,"
James said.

Major Waldron stroked his chin for a moment
before speaking again. "I ought to warn you,
though, the Bozeman Trail goes right through
the middle of Sioux Indian territory. And the
Sioux aren't known for their hospitality toward
whites, if you get my meanin'."

"I understand," James said. "We'll be
careful."

When the Confederate cavalry pulled out half
an hour later, Matthew, Mark, Luke, and John
ran alongside the departing column, holding up
whiskey jugs, selling "one last drink" for a dollar, and finding takers. Major Waldron saw what
was going on and ordered his men to proceed
at the gallop, thus leaving temptation behind.

"You fellas come on back!" Matthew called to
the departing soldiers. He held the jug up. "You
goin' to have a long dry spell!" he shouted.

When none of the soldiers answered his call,
Matthew took one final drink himself, then
corked the jug.

"Well, that was twenty dollars, just as slick as a whistle," Mark said.

"Wisht we could run into some more soldier-boys," Luke said.

"We keep on goin' north, the next soldier-boys we run in to is liable to be Yankees," John suggested.

"Don't make no never mind to us," Matthew said. "They all drink whiskey."

The others laughed.

James shook his head in disgust. They were driving thousands of dollars' worth of cows to market, and the Scattergoods were concerned about twenty dollars' worth of whiskey.

"If Revelation hadn't got them two boys to fightin' over her, we could'a made us a lot more," Mark said.

Mark's comment about his sister reminded James that he wanted to speak to her, to caution her against any future incidents of the kind she caused with her careless flirtation with the soldiers. He walked back to her wagon.

"Revelation, just what did you mean by causing all that commotion before?" James asked, even before he peeked into the wagon. "Don't you know that—?" James's question died on his lips when he looked in, because he caught her changing clothes. The dress she had been wearing was now lying across a sack of flour. She was wearing nothing but a camisole and underdrawers. Her long shapely legs were bare.

"Oh, excuse me!" James said, turning away from the wagon in embarrassment.

"I'll be with you in a moment," Revelation said, obviously unperturbed by the interruption.

"I'm sorry, Miss Scattergood," James said. "I didn't men to intrude like that."

"Miss Scattergood, is it?" Revelation asked, a moment later. "When did you start calling me Miss Scattergood? You've been calling me Revelation for the entire drive."

"I guess I just never thought of you as a woman before," James said.

"And now?" Revelation asked, obviously flirting with him. "How do you think of me now?"

James cleared his throat. "I think you could be a troublemaker," he said. "I would appreciate it if, in the future you, uh . . ." He turned back toward her.

"Yes, Mr. Cason?" Revelation asked. Bending over to pick up her trousers, she presented a generous spill of breasts above her camisole. "If I would what?"

Closing his eyes, James turned away again. "If you would make a less obvious display of your, uh, gender."

Revelation chuckled, amused by James's discomfort. "I will do what I can, Mr. Cason," she said.

Chapter Eleven

With the Golden Calf Cattle Company, mile 450,
Saturday, July 19, 1862:

The herd crossed into Indian Territory going as
far as the Canadian River without encountering
any difficulty with the Indians. They saw them
often enough, but they were never in groups of
more than three or four and they gave no sign
of hostility.

But when they made camp on the Canadian,
Luke and John sneaked out after everyone else
was in bed. The next morning the two Scattergood brothers were brought into camp, in
irons, escorted by Indian Police who had arrested them for attempting to sell whiskey.

After some negotiation, the Indians agreed to
accept ten cows as payment for the fine.

"Bob, Billy, cut ten Scattergood cows out of
the herd," James ordered.

"Wait a minute," Matthew protested. "You

can't do that! If you're goin' to pay these heathen ten cows, it's got to come out of everyone's herd equal."

"Everyone didn't try and sell whiskey to the Indians," James said.

"All right, even so, it was Luke and John that done it, not me 'n Mark. You got no right makin' us pay for what they done."

"You are all in this together," James insisted.

"Well, I don't intend to just stand by an' let you take ten of our cows."

"Oh, I think you will," Duke said easily.

"What have you got to do with this conversation?" Matthew challenged.

"Like James said, we're all in this together. Now, I didn't try and sell any whiskey to the Indians, so if we're goin' to have to pay them off, we aren't paying them with any of my cows. I'm pretty sure Billy and Bob feel the same way. That leaves your cows."

Though Duke was speaking quietly, his challenge was open and direct. And in some strange way, the fact that it was soft-spoken, made it all the more frightening.

"Yeah, well, it don't seem in no way right to me," Matthew said, but his tone of voice indicated that he wouldn't carry his protest any further.

To the surprise of James and his friends, the Scattergoods generally held up their end of the bargain, each of them working as hard as any of those in James's original party. What wasn't a surprise to them was the fact that Revelation was working the hardest of all.

When the drovers were finished with their supper, they would sit around the campfire, smoking their pipes, telling stories, and stretching weary muscles. While they were relaxing in such a way, Revelation, who had already put in a full day's work, would be cleaning up from supper. Later, when the men would crawl wearily into bedrolls, reeking with their own musk, Revelation would still be up, making preparations for the next day's meals.

Then, when the drovers awakened the next morning, the air would be permeated with the rich smell of coffee brewing, bacon frying, and biscuits baking. That was because Revelation, who didn't go to bed until about an hour after the last drover had drifted off to sleep, also rose an hour before anyone else. And finally, even before the herd began to move, Revelation would have the wagon loaded, the team harnessed and the wheels rolling as she forged on ahead, looking for the next campsite.

The hardest part of the drive was to get the cows moving each morning. The campsites were picked where there was plenty of grass and water. In addition, there would be an occasional tree or an overhanging bluff to provide some respite from the sun, so the cows were reluctant to leave. Every morning they showed all intentions of staying right where they were.

Sometimes the drovers would have to shout, probe the animals with sticks, and swing their ropes to get the herd underway. Eventually their efforts would pay off, and the herd would begin to move. Then, once the herd was underway, it would change from three thousand–plus individual creatures into a single entity with a single purpose. The inertia they needed to overcome to get the herd moving in the first place, now worked in their favor as the cows would plod along all day long at a steady clip, showing no inclination to stop.

There was a distinctive smell to a herd this size. The smells came from sun on the hides, dust in the air, and especially from the animals' droppings and urine. The odor was pungent and perhaps, to many, unpleasant. To James, however, it was an aroma as familiar and agreeable as the smell of flour and cinnamon on his mother's apron.

It had been a long, hard journey so far, and they had even farther to go. But as far as James was concerned, there was no place in the world he would rather be than right here, right now.

Revelation Scattergood's cooking skills had been a pleasant surprise. Though she dressed, rode, and worked as hard as any man, she showed a woman's touch in the kitchen. Often she would surprise the men, who were used to trail grub, with something a little special.

Tonight it was apple pie, and as she served everyone supper, James noticed that she had given him an extra-large piece of pie.

"No, this is too large," he said, holding his tin plate back toward her. "I don't want to cheat the other men."

"You aren't cheating them," Revelation said. "I'm giving you my piece."

"Why would you do that?"

"Maybe it's because I like the way you stood up to my brothers," Revelation said. She smiled. "Or, maybe it's because I like you," she added.

"Well, I, uh, I appreciate it," James said, not knowing what else to say.

Over the next several days, it became obvious, even to the others, that Revelation had her sights set on making James Cason her man. James tried to ignore it as much as he could, but Bob, Billy, and Duke wouldn't allow it. They found every opportunity to tease him.

"Bob, you got a suit and tie?" Billy Swan asked one day, when the four of them were together.

"Yes, I have a suit and tie."

"What about you, Duke? You got one?"

Duke shook his head. "I've never owned one," he said. "What would I need one for?"

"Why, for the wedding," Billy answered.

"What wedding?"

"The wedding between James and Revelation," Billy said. "Way things are looking, they'll be getting married soon as we get back to Texas, and I reckon we'll be wanting to go."

"Ha!" Bob said. "The way things are going, they'll be getting married before we get back to Texas. Probably in the next little town we come to."

"Well, in that case, I won't be needing a suit after all, will I?" Duke asked. "All I'll need is a pair of clean denim trousers and maybe a new shirt."

Everyone but James laughed.

"That's about enough of all that," James said.

"You may as well face it, James. That girl is in love with you."

"All I can say is, you boys have a very active imagination," James said. "She's just being nice, that's all."

"Uh-huh. You just keep telling yourself that," Billy said. "That's how it works, you know. Women are a lot smarter than men when it comes to things like that. A woman will set her cap for a man and the next thing you know, she's got him throwed, hog-tied, and branded before he knows what hit him."

Snorting in disgust, James rode away from the others as their laughter followed him.

Mile 645,
Thursday, July 31, 1862:

They reached the Arkansas River after seven weeks on the trail. The lead animals bawled and refused the ford at first, but the drovers forced them in. Then, once the herd was started across the water it again became one entity, with all the trailing cows following without protest.

With his leg hooked across the pommel of his saddle, James sat astride his horse on the south bank and watched as the stream of animals moved down into the water. Their hooves made clacking sounds on the rocky bank of the river, and their longhorns rattled as they came in contact with each other.

He could see the ribs on each cow as it plunged into the water, and he was struck with how lean they were. It wasn't so much that they weren't getting enough to eat, as it was that they were trail-lean. They had literally walked all the pounds off of them. At this rate they would reach Dakota with nothing but tough and stringy animals. He wasn't sure how much they would be able to charge for such animals, or even if anyone would be interested in buying them.

Once the entire herd was across, he called everyone together.

"We've probably walked off half the tallow

over the last seven weeks. Because of that, I think we should stay here for a few days to recruit our animals," James said. "We've plenty of water and grass, and I have a feeling the hardest part of the drive is before us."

Although James was the trail boss, he wanted, when possible, to do things by consensus. Thus it was that he gave everyone an equal opportunity to speak. To his relief, everyone, even the Scattergoods, agreed with him.

The Texans' cow camp was less than three miles from Fort Larned, Kansas. Leaving Bob, Billy, Matthew, and Mark to watch over the herd, James, Duke, Luke, and John rode to the fort. There was a small settlement just outside the fort itself. The town appeared to consist almost entirely of saloons, brothels, and gaming houses, primarily as a means of relieving the soldiers of their monthly pay.

"Well now, lookie here," Luke said, smiling broadly as he looked up at several of the prostitutes who were leaning over the railing of an upstairs balcony. "I do believe I'm going to enjoy this place."

"Stay out of trouble," James cautioned.

"I ain't lookin' for trouble," Luke said. "I'm just lookin' for a little fun."

Luke and John stopped in front of one of the saloons. James rode on for a few more yards before he realized they were no longer riding with him. He stopped and looked back toward them as they were tying their horses to the hitch rail. It was obvious that they were eager to get inside.

"Maybe you'd better stay with them, Duke," James said. "Keep them out of trouble, if you can."

"You don't need me with you?"

"No, I'm just going to see what kind of information I can get from the post commander about the trail ahead. As soon as I talk to him, I'll join you."

"All right, I'll watch them for you." He smiled. "Besides, a beer would taste awfully good right now," Duke said.

James left the three men in front of one of the saloons, then he rode up to Fort Larned.* When he reached the front gate, a guard stepped in front of him, bringing his rifle to port arms.

"State your name and your business, mister," the guard said.

"My name is James Cason. I'm a cattleman, here to see the commanding officer."

The guard called the sergeant of the guard, who came to give James the once-over. Finally the sergeant nodded. "All right, tie your horse over there," he said, pointing to a hitching rail, "then come with me."

---

*Established in 1859 to protect the Santa Fe Trail.

* * *

The post was garrisoned by Company H of the Twelfth Kansas Volunteer Infantry. The commanding officer, who was a lawyer in civilian life, was Captain Lawrence Appleby.

"You say you are a cattleman?" Appleby asked, when James was brought to him.

"Yes. I'm driving a herd north, from Texas to Dakota."

Appleby looked up sharply, when he heard the word Texas.

"From Texas, you say?"

"That's right. My folks own a ranch in Bexar County, near San Antonio."

Appleby stroked his chin as he studied James. "Technically—Mr. Cason, is it?—that makes you an enemy."

"I don't know how that could be. I haven't taken up arms against the United States."

"But you are a Texan, and Texas is one of the states in rebellion."

"The government of the state of Texas may be in rebellion, but I am not," James said. "If I were, I would have joined the army of the Confederacy."

"Then, perhaps you would like to join the Union army?"

"No, I wouldn't. The reason I'm here now is because I want no part of this war."

"A lot of people want no part of this war,"

Appleby said. "But there is such a thing as duty to one's country, and the honor of service."

"I don't believe it is my duty to kill my own kin," James said. "And I'm sure there's no honor in that."

"Honest men can disagree on some things, Mr. Cason. But I see little room for disagreement over service to one's country. You see, I joined the Kansas Volunteers because I *did* want to be a part of this war. Great and historical battles are being fought back East at places like Pittsburg Landing, Fredericksburg, Seven Pines, Gaines Mill."

Appleby sighed.

"And where am I during this glorious crusade? I am cooling my heels at a post so far removed from the war that I may as well be in England. And the men they have given me? They are the dregs of society, misfits every one of them. Would you believe that the desertion rate here is as high as it is in a unit that is involved in battle?"

"Why is that?"

"In a word, Mr. Cason, gold," Captain Appleby said. "In case you haven't heard, gold has been discovered in Dakota, and a number of my soldiers have left in search of their fortune. In fact, I believe some of them volunteered for duty here just so they would be closer to the gold find in Dakota. But, from all accounts, the scalps of many of these deserters now decorate Indian lodges between here and Dakota."

"That brings me to the point of my visit with you, Captain," James said. "I plan to take a new trail, called the Bozeman Trail, into Dakota. What do you know of that trail, and of the Indians there?"

"As it so happens, Mr. Cason, Fort Larned is the location of the agency for the Cheyenne and Arapaho Indians. Therefore we get many reports from this so-called Bozeman Trail. And I can tell you this. The establishment of that trail has violated every accord we ever had with the Indians. It goes right through their territory and they are not happy about it. Many a traveler has been attacked while taking that trail to the gold fields of Dakota," Captain Appleby said. "I strongly advise you not to go that way. In fact, my advice to you would be not to go any farther at all."

"Are you suggesting that I turn around and take my herd back to Texas?" James asked.

"I'm suggesting that you turn around, yes. But you needn't take your herd back to Texas. You could sell your cows to the army. I'm sure my quartermaster will pay you a fair amount. Not in cash, of course, but with a voucher that will be redeemable from the government in Washington."

"What does your quartermaster consider a fair amount?"

"Twenty dollars a head."

"That's less than half of what I can get for them in Dakota. Thank you, but no, I think we will go on."

"You can only get that much money for your cows in Dakota if you make it to Dakota," Captain Appleby said, pointedly.

"We will make it," James said. "All we need is a little help."

"Help? Mr. Cason, you aren't asking for a military escort, are you?"

"Actually, all I was going to ask for was a copy of the latest maps of the area," James said. "But I would be a fool to turn a military escort down, if such is available."

"Under ordinary circumstances, a military escort might be available to you. But these aren't ordinary circumstances. There is a war on, and you, and I take it the others with you on this drive, are Texans. How would it look in the press if some of my men were killed while providing an escort for Southerners?"

"It probably wouldn't look very good," James said in agreement.

"I could wire back to Fort Leavenworth and request permission to provide an escort. I don't think they will give me approval, and there is even a possibility that they will order me to detain you and confiscate your herd. Would you like me to send that wire?"

"No," James said.

"I didn't think you would. So, what are you going to do, Mr. Cason? Are you going to try and go on alone? Or, shall I send for my quartermaster to buy your herd?"

"I'm going on," James said, resolutely.

"I wish you luck," Appleby said, by way of dismissal.

The Bucket of Blood Saloon:

Duke and John were standing at the bar, having a drink. Luke was with them, but he was paying more attention to one of the prostitutes than he was to his beer. Four soldiers were sitting at a nearby table.

"Hey, where you fellas from?" one of the soldiers asked.

"We're from—" John started, but Duke interrupted him.

"We're from a cow camp up the river a short distance," Duke said. "We're driving a herd of cattle through here."

"Yeah, well, what I mean is, where did you bring them cows from?"

"Texas," John answered before Duke could cut him off.

Duke sighed, because John's answer had just the effect he was trying to avoid.

"Texas? By God, you mean to tell me you Rebel bastards got the sand to come up here?"

"We're from Texas, but we're not Rebels," Duke said.

"You ain't, huh? Well, you look like Rebels to me," the soldier insisted.

"How the hell would you know what a Rebel looks like?" John asked. "You ain't exactly in the middle of the war out here."

"I say you three pukes are Rebels," the soldier said, getting up from his chair. "And I'm tellin' you to go on back to where you came from."

Without saying another word, John threw his beer mug at the soldier. He missed the soldier who was his target, but he hit one of the other soldiers sitting at the same table.

One of the soldiers at the table threw his own beer mug and it sailed by John and Duke, smashing several bottles of liquor that were sitting on a shelf behind the bar.

With that, the fight was on. Other soldiers joined the first group, giving them a three-to-one edge over the cowboys. Tables were broken and chairs were splintered as the fight grew in intensity.

James was just walking toward the saloon to

meet the others, when the window suddenly exploded into a shower of glass as a chair came flying outside. From inside the saloon he could hear angry shouts and curses, and he realized at once what was happening. He ran into the saloon with his gun drawn. Stepping through the door, he saw three soldiers lying on the floor. A fourth soldier was on his knees, shaking his head as if trying to clear away the cobwebs. Five soldiers were still on their feet, however, and they were closing a circle around the three cowboys.

"Hold it!" James shouted. When nobody paid any attention to him, he shouted again, firing his pistol at the same time. The gunshot boomed through the saloon and a heavy cloud of smoke and the acrid smell of spent powder drifted through the room.

The gunshot had the desired effect of getting everyone's attention and all activity came to a halt.

"Now, you soldier-boys just back on away from my pards, there," James ordered, making a little waving motion with his pistol.

The soldiers moved a few feet away from the bar. Their hands were up and they were glaring at James.

"All the way," James said. "Go over to that table in the far corner and sit down."

Grumbling, the soldiers did as ordered.

"Now, Duke, take these two with you on outside, get on your horses and go back to camp," James said.

Duke and Luke started to comply, but John turned back to the bar.

"You boys go on. I ain't goin' nowhere 'till I've finished my drink and had me a woman," he said.

Almost imperceptibly, James nodded at Duke. Slipping his pistol from his holster, Duke hit John just behind the ear. John went down, and Duke scooped him up. Then, carrying John over his shoulder, Duke followed Luke outside.

With his gun still pointed toward the soldiers, including the ones on the floor who were just now beginning to regain their feet, James backed out of the saloon.

"Hey!" the saloon proprietor shouted. "Who's going to pay for the damage to my place? I've got a broke window, couple of busted chairs, and a dozen bottles of liquor ruined here."

"How much?"

"A hundred dollars for sure."

"We've got a cow camp about three miles upriver," James said. "I'll cut out five head and leave them tied to a tree. You can come up and get them. Will that satisfy you?"

The proprietor nodded. "If I find five cows tied to a tree, I'll be satisfied."

James was the last to leave, still holding his

gun at the ready as he backed through the door.
A moment later, those in the saloon heard the
sound of hoofbeats as the cowboys rode off.

Private Murphy, who was one of the soldiers
ordered to the table, got up quickly and started
toward the door.

"I wouldn't do that if I were you, soldier," the
proprietor said. "That fool cowboy might just be
waiting for someone to stick his head through
the door so he can shoot it off. I know them
Texans."

Murphy halted his charge toward the door.
He went over to the bar. There were the ghosts
of missing stripes on Murphy's sleeve, indicating that his present rank of private was the result of some misdeed in the past. Picking up
what was left of John Scattergood's beer, he
drank it.

"Say, will them cows really pay for the damage that was done in here?" he asked.

"They sure will. There is a standing offer from
the U.S. Army for cattle. They'll pay twenty dollars apiece for 'em."

"Is that a fact?" Murphy asked.

"What does the army want with cattle?" one
of the other soldiers asked.

"What does the army want with cattle? Where
do you think we get our beef?" Murphy replied.

"Seems to me like we don't hardly ever have
none," the first soldier said. "Seems to me,

mostly all we get is beans and, sometimes, a little bacon."

"What with the war on and all, there's a lot more soldiers than there is beef available," the saloon proprietor explained. "And what beef is available goes to the fightin' men, not soldier-boys like you, safe in some distant fort. That's why there is a standing order for cattle, and the army is willing to pay good money to anyone who can furnish them with beef."

Murphy walked back to the table to sit with the others. "Twenty dollars for one cow. Did you fellas hear that?"

"Yeah, I heard it," one of the other soldiers said. "Twenty dollars is damn near two months' pay."

"That's a lot of money," another soldier said.

"You know, if we had us, say, a hundred cows, that would be worth some real money," Murphy said.

"Yeah, if we had a hundred cows."

Murphy smiled at the others. "Well, I know where we can get a hundred cows," he said.

"Where?"

"Didn't you hear that Texan tell the barkeep that he had a cow camp just up the river a ways? A cow camp means there's cows."

"Are you suggesting we rustle cattle?" one of the others asked.

"Nah," Murphy said, dismissing the suggestion with a wave of his hand. "It wouldn't be rustling. We're in the Union army, them boys are Rebels. All we would be doing is confiscating a few cows for the government."

"What's the good of that? If we confiscated them for the army, the army would just take them away from us and we'd get nothing."

"Yeah," another agreed. "And it don't matter what they are paying civilians to sell them beef—they ain't going to pay soldiers."

"I was thinking we could sell the cows to the barkeep, then he could sell them to the army."

"Think he'd do that?"

"I'll give you boys fifteen dollars a head," the barkeep said, overhearing their conversation.

Chapter Twelve

Cow camp on the Arkansas River, early morning, Friday, August 1, 1862:

Billy Swan was riding Nighthawk when he heard the faint sound of hooves on rock. Since the herd was at rest, he looked around to find the source of the sound and saw a long dark line, ragged with heads and horns, moving away from the main herd.

It took him a moment to realize exactly what was happening, but once he figured it out, he reacted quickly.

"Cattle thieves!" he shouted. "James, Bob, Duke, the rest of you, wake up! Turn out! We're being robbed!"

Billy's shout not only awakened his partners, it alerted the thieves and, instantly one of them fired a shot at the sound of Billy's voice. Billy saw the muzzle flash, then heard the bullet whiz by, amazingly close for a wild shot in the dark.

Billy shot back, and the crack of the guns right over the heads of the pilfered cows started them running. By now, rapid fire began coming from the camp itself as James and the others rolled out of their blankets and began shooting. Revelation was standing in the wagon, firing a rifle, adding her own effort to the fight.

Billy put his pistol away and raised his rifle. He aimed toward the dust and the swirling melee of cattle, waiting for one of the robbers to present a target. One horse appeared, but its saddle was empty. Then another horse appeared, this time with a rider who was shooting wildly.

Billy fired and the robber's horse broke stride, then fell, carrying his rider down with him, right in front of the running cattle. Downed horse and rider disappeared under the hooves of the maddened beasts.

"Let's go! Let's get out of here!" someone shouted.

"What about the cattle?" another voice asked.

"Leave 'em! They're runnin' wild; we'll never get 'em under control now!"

As nearly as Billy could tell, there were three remaining rustlers, or would-be rustlers, and they started off, running in the opposite direction from the running cows.

Billy was torn between a desire to go after the rustlers or run down the cattle. So far, only the cattle that had been stolen were running. The main herd, though made restless by the flashes and explosions in the night, milled around but resisted running.

James appeared alongside Billy at that moment, now mounted on his own horse.

"Let's get them back!" James shouted to Billy, indicating they should go after the running cows.

"What about the rest of the herd?"

"Bob and the others will keep the herd here," James said, spurring his horse into a gallop toward the fleeing cows.

Billy urged his own horse into a gallop, and within a minute he and James were riding alongside the lumbering animals.

"We've got to get to the front!" James called.

The cows were running as fast as they could, which was about three quarters of the speed of the horses. But what the cattle lacked in speed, they made up for with their momentum. With lowered heads, wild eyes, and flopping tongues, the cattle ran as if there were no tomorrow.

Finally, James and Billy reached the head of the column, rode to the front and were able to turn them. Once the cows were turned, they lost their forward momentum, slowed their running to a trot, and finally to a walk. When that happened, James and Billy were able to turn them around and start them back.

Fifteen minutes later they brought the small herd back. Bob, Duke, and the Scattergoods, including Revelation, had been able to keep the main herd calm. When the one hundred would-be rustled cows were returned to the others, everything settled down once more.

"Who was that?" James asked, getting down from his horse. "Who tried to rustle cows from us? It wasn't Indians, was it?"

Bob shook his head. "It was soldiers," he said.

"Soldiers?"

"At least the two we killed were soldiers."

"Damn, I hate that," James said. "That's bound to cause trouble with the army."

"I don't know why it should cause trouble," Bob said. "After all, they were the ones who were doing the stealing."

James, Billy, and Duke went over to look down at the two dead soldiers. One of them was unmarked, except for a bullet hole in his forehead, just above the right eye. The other soldier was so badly mangled, bruised, and practically dismembered by the hooves of the cattle that the body was barely recognizable as that of a human being.

"James, do you recognize this fella?" Duke asked then. He had been looking at the less damaged of the two bodies.

"Yeah," James said. "Yeah, I do recognize him. He's one of the ones we saw in the bar."

"Yes, his name was Murphy, I think."

"Yankee bastard, serves him right," John said.

"What do we do now?" Bob asked.

"Now we break camp," James said. "I don't think the soldiers we ran into are going to be in any hurry to report to their superiors what just happened here." He pointed to the two bodies. "But they are going to have to account for these two men soon. So I suggest we get going."

"What do you mean, get going?" Matthew complained. "Me 'n Mark didn't even get a chance to go into town."

"The way things are right now, if you go into town you are likely to stay there," James said. "Either in jail, or shot down by some other soldiers."

"Yeah, well, this ain't no way right," Matthew complained. "I mean, some folks getting to go into town and some folks not."

"What are going to do about them two?" Bob asked, nodding toward the two dead soldiers. "Think we should bury them?"

James shook his head. "No. Once the army realizes they are missing, they'll come looking for them. If we bury them, it'll make it hard for them to find them."

"Once they do find them, they're goin' to know what happened to them, then they'll come looking for us," Matthew Scattergood said.

"That's true," James said. "That's why I want to get out of here now."

"All right, you heard the man," Bob said. "Let's get going."

"What about breakfast?" Matthew asked.

"What about it?" James replied.

"Well, we ain't et yet, that's what about it," Matthew said, complaining bitterly.

"We'll eat in the saddle, jerky and water," James said. "Come on, let's go. I want to be five miles away from here by the time the sun comes up."

Fort Benton on the Missouri, Friday, August 1, 1862:

Fort Benton was established by the American Fur Company as a trading post in 1845. Named after Senator Thomas Hart Benton of Missouri, it was at the absolute head of steam navigation on the Missouri River, and the fastest way into the Northwest territories. During the gold rush of 1862, it became an exceptionally busy port.

Landing a riverboat in the shallow waters at Fort Benton required a great deal of teamwork between the captain, leadsman, engine room, and deckhands. The boat had to be maneuvered around sand shoals and over sunken obstacles, all the while maintaining enough power to over-come the powerful current. With the relief valve booming like cannonfire, and the wheel working the water into a muddy frenzy, the *River Queen* made ready to land.

Angus, Chance, and Percy Butrum stood on the hurricane deck, watching the activity as the boat put in at Fort Benton. It landed by ramming its bow into the bank, then maintained that position by tying a hawser around a tree.

"Ain't much of a town," Percy said, looking at the low-lying, gray, rip-sawed buildings scattered along the bank of the river.

"What did you expect? St. Louis?" Angus asked. "We ain't plannin' on settlin' here. All we want is to settle up with Mr. Duke Faglier, then get our hands on some of that gold we've been hearin' about. Once we do that, we can take a boat back East and live high and fine."

"Don't forget, there's still a war goin' on back East," Chance said.

"Won't make no never mind to us, we ain't goin' to be a-fightin' it. And iff'en a body is smart, he can make a lot of money durin' a war. But you got to have money to make money and that's why we come out here."

When the boat crew lowered a gangplank down from the bow to the riverbank, the Butrum brothers were the first passengers off the boat.

"Where do we go now?" Percy asked, scratching his crotch as he stood at the top of the riverbank, looking around at the small gray town.

"What about findin' us some women?" Chance suggested.

"You see any women here?" Percy asked.

Although the main street of the little town was crowded with people, there was not one woman to be seen.

"I'll be damned," Chance said, as if noticing that fact for the first time. "You're right. There ain't a woman nowhere."

"Well, while you two is discussin' somethin' that you can't do nothin' about, I plan to look into somethin' I can do somethin' about," Angus said. "I'm goin' to have a drink."

"Where you reckon a saloon is?" Percy asked.

"Hell, it ought not to be hard to find one. Just follow your nose," Angus replied.

Finding something to drink wasn't all that difficult. Every other building, it seemed, was a saloon. With no predetermined purpose in mind, other than to find drink, the Butrums headed toward one of them. A crudely painted sign out front identified the establishment as the "North Star."

Although it was early afternoon, the saloon was crowded with noisy customers. A piano sat in the back of the saloon, with a sign that read, THIS PIANO WAS BROUGHT UPRIVER FROM ST. LOUIS ABOARD THE RIVERBOAT, *MISSOURI MIST*. IT IS THE ONLY PIANO IN THE ENTIRE TERRITORY. PLEASE TREAT IT WITH CARE.

Despite the printed plea, the instrument was marked with half a dozen cigar burns and glass-rings, and punctured with three bullet holes.

"Bartender, give me a bottle!" one of the customers said, shouting to be heard above the din. The bartender pulled a bottle from a shelf behind the bar, handed it to the customer, then accepted as payment a pinch of gold dust. Percy watched the operation, then excitedly punched his brother.

"Angus! Did you see how that fella paid for his whiskey?"

"No."

"With a pinch of gold dust from a bag he's carryin'," Percy said.

After Percy's disclosure, the three brothers began paying more attention to the business going on around them. To their amazement, more than half of all purchases were being made with gold dust.

"Damn!" Angus said. "What they said about findin' gold up here must be true!"

"Look at that fella over there," Angus said, pointing to a man at the other end of the bar. His pouch of gold dust was bulging, but that wasn't the only thing of interest about him. He was also very drunk.

The Butrum brothers watched the drunk until he started outside. They exited the saloon just behind him.

As the drunk staggered down the boardwalk, Angus and Chance followed close behind. In the meantime, Percy ran across the street, then hurried to get ahead of the drunk. Recrossing the street, he started back toward the drunk so that their mark was now between Percy and his two brothers.

"Hey, friend," Percy said, accosting the drunk as they came together, "could you tell me where the nearest saloon is?"

The drunk chuckled. "Are you blind, mister?" he asked. He made an unsteady wave with his hand. "They are all around here, on both sides of the stre—" That was as far as he got. Angus hit him just behind the ear with the butt of his pistol. The drunk would have fallen, had Chance not caught him. Quickly, the three dragged their victim to a small open space in between the nearest two buildings. Once they had him off the street, Angus reached down to relieve him of his pouch of gold dust.

"I got it!" Angus said, triumphantly.

"How much is there?" Percy asked.

"Enough to buy about anything we want," Angus replied.

"About the only thing that's going to buy you boys is some time in jail," another voice said.

Gasping in surprise at being caught, the three brothers stood up from their victim, and found themselves looking into the barrel of a pistol.

"Sheriff Plummer is going to be real pleased to see you boys," the man holding the gun said. "I'm his deputy."

"George, is that you? George Ives?" Angus asked, studying the man who was holding the gun.

The deputy blinked in surprise. "Do you know me, mister?"

"If you're the George Ives from Missouri, I know you. You used to be good friends with our brother, Mingus Butrum. I'm Angus, these here are my two brothers, Chance and Percy."

"I'll be damned," Ives said. He laughed. "Yes, Mingus and I drank from the same bottle many times before I left Missouri. How's that old mule doing?"

The smile left Angus's face. "He was killed by a no 'count polecat by the name of Duke Faglier."

Ives shook his head. "Faglier? I don't think I know him."

"Didn't none of us know him. He was a farm boy from Clay County. The son of a bitch killed two of my brothers, not only Mingus, but Frank, too."

"I hope you took care of him," Ives said.

"We ain't yet, but we aim to," Angus said. "That's why we come out here."

"He's out here?"

"He's comin' here," Percy said.

"Yeah, bringin' a herd of cows," Chance added. "You ever heard of anything so dumb?"

"I don't know," Ives said. "Maybe it's not so dumb. There could be a lot of money in something like that."

"Are you really a deputy sheriff?" Angus asked.

Ives laughed. "Yeah," he said. "Well, sort of. Oh, where are my manners?" He put his gun away, then stuck his hand out to shake hands with Angus.

"What do you mean, sort of?" Angus asked. "Either you are a deputy or you ain't."

"Well, I'm deputing for a man named Henry Plummer, who ain't really a sheriff yet but intends to be one sometime soon.* In the meantime, he's formed something he calls the Bannack Mining District Vigilance Committee. And he's appointed himself sheriff. Say, maybe you'd like to join us. I'll put in a good word with Sheriff Plummer, if you'd like."

Angus shook his head. "No thanks. I wasn't cut out to be no deputy sheriff."

"Don't be so quick to turn it down. It ain't like you think," Ives said. "For example, this pouch of gold you boys just took? Well, now, half of it will go to Henry Plummer, him bein' the sheriff and all. He'll call it a fine against that

*Henry Plummer wasn't elected sheriff of the Bannack Mining District Vigilance Committee until May of 1863

fella for bein' drunk. But I get to keep the other half as a reward for findin' it. Only, if you'd like to join up with us, why, I'll let you boys have it. Believe me, there's plenty more where this came from."

"Wait a minute," Percy said. "What do you mean, you will let us keep half of it? It ain't up to you to give us nothin'. Hell, we the ones that took it in the first place. It's all ours."

"Do you think so?" Ives asked.

"Don't pay no attention to Percy, George," Angus said quickly. He glared at his brother. "I'll take care of him. We'll be glad to join up with you."

"You'll join up with us iff'n I can talk Sheriff Plummer into agreein' to take you," Ives said, glaring at Percy. "And with that kind of attitude, I don't know as he will."

"You take care of the sheriff, I'll take care of my brother," Angus promised.

Chapter Thirteen

*With the Golden Calf Cattle Company,
mile 752
Friday, August 8, 1862:*

From the moment they left Long Shadow, the possibility of a stampede was always in the back of everyone's mind. The problem was, nobody could predict when a stampede might occur. Sometimes they would be so stable that not even a close-strike lightning bolt could set them off. At other times they could be startled by the snap of a twig.

The most effective way to stop a stampede was to have the flank rider on each side gradually turn the cows in front until they were moving in a wide circle. If a rider on one side saw the herd turning his way, then he would fall back and let the man on the other side tighten the turn of the leaders until he, too, was in position to help. Once the cows were running in a circle, they would run themselves down.

On this day, there had been no water since early in the morning, and they had pushed the herd hard to get them through a long dry passage. The cows were hot, tired, and thirsty. They began to get a little restless, and James and the others who were working around the perimeters were kept busy keeping them moving.

Then, at about three o'clock in the afternoon, Matthew Scattergood saw a rattlesnake.

"Rattler!" he shouted, as he pulled his pistol.

"No, Matthew, don't!" Bob called to him.

Despite James's warning, Matthew fired at the rattlesnake and, missing it, fired again and again, until the pistol was empty. Frightened, the cows jumped, then began to run. The terror spread throughout the herd and, like a wild prairie fire before the wind, the herd ran out of control.

"Stampede! Stampede!"

The warning was first issued by Bob, then picked up by the others, though as the herd was now in full gallop, there was no longer any need to issue the call.

"Stampede!"

Although there was terror in the cry, there was grim determination, too, for every man who issued the cry moved quickly to do what he could do to stop it.

James was riding in the right flank position when the herd started. Fortunately for him, the herd started to the left, a living tidal wave of thundering hoofbeats, millions of pounds of muscle and bone, horn and hair, red eyes and running noses. Over three thousand animals welded together as one, gigantic, raging beast.

A cloud of dust rose up from the herd and billowed high into the air. The air was so thick with it that within moments James could see nothing. It was as if he were caught in the thickest fog one could imagine, but this fog was brown and it burned the eyes and clogged the nostrils and stung the face with its fury.

James managed to overtake the herd, then seeing that the front had veered to the left, proceeded to tighten the turn, attempting to force them into a great churning circle. The cowboys were shouting and whistling and waving their hats and ropes at the herd, trying to get them to respond. That was when James caught, just out of the corner of his eye, Mark Scattergood falling from his horse. The stampeding cows altered their rush just enough to come toward the hapless cowboy and he stood up and tried to outrun them, though it was clear that he was going to lose the race.

James tried to get to him but it was too late. The herd rolled over him and Mark went down. If Mark screamed, his cry was drowned out by clacking horns and thundering hooves that shook the ground. James had time for only a passing thought as to Mark's fate, before he turned back to the business at hand.

Finally, under the relentless pressure of the cowboys, the herd was twisted into a giant circle. They continued to run in the circle until, finally, they tired and slowed from a mad dash to a brisk trot, then from a trot to a walk. The stampede had at last run itself out, brought under control by the courage and will of a few determined men. An aggregate total of less than fifteen hundred pounds of men were once more in control of nearly two million pounds of cattle.

They buried Mark Scattergood's mangled body under a small scrub tree, not too far from where he fell. Even as they were walking away from his grave, Luke and John were in an argument over his clothes.

"That there red-and-blue shirt of his'n is mine," Luke insisted.

"What do you mean it's yours?" John asked.

"'Cause Mark hisself told me," Luke said. "He said, Luke, if'n anythin' ever happens to me, I want you to have my red-and-blue shirt."

"You're a lyin' son of a bitch. He never said such a thing."

"Yes, he did."

"Well, it don't matter none, anyhow. You can have the shirt. I want his boots."

"I want his pocketknife."

"Listen to you two," Revelation said, scolding them. "Mark isn't cold in his grave yet, and you two are fighting over his things. Can't you feel a moment of sorrow over his death?"

"Don't know why you so broke up over it," Luke said.

"Because he was our brother," Revelation said. "Can't you understand that?"

Luke and John looked at Revelation for a long moment, then John looked at Luke. "I get the saddle," he said, completely ignoring his sister's remarks.

"The hell you do. That saddle is mine," Luke replied.

Realizing that her admonition had meant nothing to them, Revelation shook her head and walked away from her quarreling brothers.

Twenty miles northwest of the present location of the herd, with the Meechum Party Wednesday, August 13, 1862:

The wagon train was called the Meechum Party because it was under the command of Captain Louis Meechum. It was quite small when compared to the wagon trains of a decade earlier. Then, trains of more than one hundred wagons were not unusual. This train consisted of only twenty wagons.

The Meechum Party was one month out of Omaha, bound for Dakota, not for gold but for land. As the steel-rimmed wheels rolled across the hard-packed earth, they kicked up dirt, causing a rooster tail of dust to stream out behind them. The wood of the wagons was bleached white, and under the sun it gave off a familiar smell.

Young Millie Parker sat in the sun on the dried seat of the wagon, reading over the latest entry in her journal.

The Magnificent Adventure
of the Parker Family
by

Millie Parker, age 16

Our days begin before dawn. The wagons have been drawn into a circle for the night, because Captain Meechum says this is the most convenient way of encampment. We are greeted each morning with the whistles and shouts of those who have been standing the last hours of the night watch.

Sometimes I like to wake up early so I can watch as the men and women begin emerging from their night-quarters. It is interesting to watch the new day start.

Some sleep inside the wagons, but these are mostly very young children. Most sleep under the wagons. That's where I sleep. Sometimes it is hard to get up in the morning, but we do it for we know we must get to our new homes before winter sets in.

The livestock spend the night inside the circle of wagons. They must be milked each morning, and that is the responsibility of the children.

I help the other women prepare the breakfast meal, which is eaten between the hours of six and seven. The men and older boys are busy during that time, too, connecting teams to the wagons, striking the tents, loading the wagons, and getting everything ready to begin the day's journey. When it is nearly time, Captain Meechum climbs onto his horse, then examines the pocket watch he carries with him. At exactly seven o'clock he lets out with a mighty roar of "Move 'em out!"

Each day we change around who shall lead and who shall ride at the rear. Today, it is our turn to be the wagon in the rear. I don't like it when it is our turn to be in the rear. If you are in the rear, dust gets in your clothes, hair, eyes, and in your nose. It is very uncomfortable, but we do it because we know that tomorrow we will go to the front and it will be several days before we work our way to the rear and have to do it again.

While we are underway, some ride in the wagons and some walk alongside. Captain Meechum rides on a magnificent horse, sometimes alongside, other times at the head, and sometimes way off, somewhere, scouting for us. The wagon train moves at a steady pace until noon. At noon, we stop for a meal and the teams are cut loose from the wagons to allow them to graze. They aren't unyoked though, and this makes it easier to get underway again when the meal is over.

By evening, humans and animals are tired. We have been on the move since before dawn, and as the sun is sinking slowly before us, we look for a suitable place to spend the night. Each night we set our guards to watch for Indians, but though we were cautioned about the savages, we have, so far, seen not so much as one Indian.

Suddenly there was a creaking, snapping sound, and the wagon lurched so badly that Millie was nearly tossed out. She looked up from her journal, startled.

"Oh!" she gasped. "What was that?"

"Whoa, team," Mrs. Parker shouted, pulling back on the reins. The team stopped and the wagon sat there, listing sharply to the right.

"Mama, what is it?" Millie asked.

"I think we've broken an axle," Mrs. Parker said grimly. "Clyde! Clyde Parker!" she called to her husband, who was walking alongside one of the wagons ahead.

The wagons in front of them, unaware that they had stopped, continued on at their same dogged pace and were slowly but surely pulling away.

"They are leaving us," Millie said.

"Clyde!" Mrs. Parker called again, and Millie added her own voice so that her father heard them and looked around.

"Louis! Louis, stop the train!" Clyde called.

Louis Meechum held up his hand and the wagons stopped. Clyde trotted back to his wagon and Meechum joined him on horseback.

"Oh damn," Clyde said as he saw the broken axle. "I was afraid of this."

"You were afraid of it," Meechum asked. "You mean you knew the possibility of breaking an axle, but you came on without changing it?"

"I knew that the axle was cracked, but I didn't want to spend the money for a new axle," Clyde said. "I was hoping it would hold."

"So, what are you going to do now?"

"Well, I did pick up a spare axle. It's used, and is cracked nearly as badly as this one. But at least it isn't completely broken. And if it will last as long as this one did, we will be there before we have any more trouble."

"How long will it take to change it?" Meechum asked.

"Oh, 'bout half a day, I reckon."

Meechum took off his hat and ran his hand through his hair. "I can't hold up the train for you. If you want to, you can unload your wagon, maybe we can find enough space in some of the other wagons for your things."

Clyde shook his head. "You know everyone is packed to the limit. No, I'm going to have to change the axle. It's going to be a long day for us, but we'll catch up with you after you've made camp tonight."

"All right," Meechum said. He looked around the horizon. "You should be all right, we haven't seen any Indians, not even any sign of them."

Mean To His Horses, an ambitious Cheyenne subchief, lay on the top of a nearby hill. He watched the wagon train pull away, leaving one wagon behind. It was obvious that the white eyes had no idea they were in danger. He slithered back down the hill to where the others were waiting.

"Did you see them?" one of the others asked.

"Yes."

"When do we attack?"

"Now."

Chapter Fourteen

With the Golden Calf Cattle Company, mile 840
Wednesday, August 13, 1862:

After supper, when Revelation had finished all
her chores, she saddled a horse and rode out
toward the herd. It took but a minute or two of
riding, and she was completely away from the
camp, swallowed up by the blue velvet of night.
The night air caressed her skin like fine silk,
while overhead the stars glistened like dia-
monds. Revelation was aware of the quiet herd,
with cows standing motionless at rest. An owl
landed nearby, his wings making a soft whirr.
He looked at Revelation with great, round,
glowing eyes, as if he had been made curious
by her passing.

The hoofbeats made soft thuds in the grass
for the next few moments until Revelation came
to a small grass-covered knoll. She could hear

the splashing, bubbling sound of the river they had been following.

Revelation dismounted and climbed to the top of the small hill so she could look down at the water just on the other side. Here, the river was fairly swift, and strewn with rocks. The water bubbled white as it tumbled over and rushed past the glistening rocks. The white feathers in the water glowed brightly in the moonlight while the water itself appeared black. The result was an exceptionally vivid contrast, which made the stream even more beautiful at night than it was by day.

Revelation felt drawn to the water, and she walked all the way down the knoll until she found a soft wide spot in the grass. There, she sat, pulling her knees up under her chin. The constant chatter of the brook soothed her, and she enjoyed the contemplative silence.

"I thought it was you I saw ride over this way," a voice said.

Revelation was startled by the sudden intrusion, and she turned to see James standing at the top of the knoll behind her.

"Aren't you supposed to be watching the herd?" Revelation asked.

"They're quiet," James said. "What are you doing out here so late."

"I couldn't sleep," Revelation answered.

"As hard as you've been working and as early as you have to get up, I can't imagine you having trouble sleeping."

"I guess I just have a lot on my mind."

"Are you thinking about Mark?"

"A little," Revelation said. "Don't get me wrong, Mark was certainly no saint. None of my brothers are. But that doesn't stop me from grieving for him." She sighed. "Besides, someone needed to. Matthew, Luke, and John didn't seem to take notice."

"I'm sorry about your brother," James said. He walked down the knoll to sit down beside her. "He turned out to be a pretty good worker. All of your brothers have."

"Which was a surprise to you, I suppose," Revelation said.

James chuckled. "Yes, it was. I admit it."

Revelation looked right at James. "What do you really know about us, Mr. James Cason, son of Colonel Garrison Cason, biggest land owner and wealthiest rancher in Bexar County?"

"Not much, I guess," James said. He was somewhat put off by the ire of her question.

"Let me tell you what you think you know. No doubt you have heard that we are a shiftless and lazy bunch. That we are cattle thieves and worse."

James cleared his throat. "I've heard words to that effect," he admitted.

"I will admit that my father and brothers have made some questionable deals in Mexico, buying cattle very cheaply without regard to how the seller came by the cattle. But they have never actually stolen any cattle, nor bought any cattle that might have been stolen from any of their neighbors."

"I guess that's something in their favor," James said.

"My mother and father were from Boston, did you know that?"

James shook his head. "No, I didn't know."

"In fact, my mother was a Prescott, an old, proud, fine family. Grandfather Prescott was in shipping. It broke his heart when mother married one of his ship captains."

James looked surprised.

"That's right. My father was a ship's captain in my grandfather's merchant fleet. But when he married my mother, my grandfather was so angry that he fired him. My grandparents pleaded with my mother to allow them to get her marriage to my father annulled, and when she refused, they disowned her. That was when my mother and father came out here."

She was silent for a moment. "You have to understand that my father was a man who was used to absolute power, for no one is more powerful than a ship's captain at sea. He was also used to the respect a ship's captain received.

"Here, he had none of that. Here, he learned that power and respect come only to those who possess land and cattle. But my father was an impatient man, as powerful men often are, and he had no interest in building his empire slowly. That is why he took shortcuts.

"I admit, that doesn't excuse him from becoming a"—Revelation couldn't bring herself to say the word cattle thief—"what he was, or causing his sons to follow in his footsteps. But it may explain a little of who he was.

"My mother died shortly after I was born. My father said she died of pneumonia, but I think she died of humiliation. She was from one of the most influential families in New England. Presidents had dined in my grandparents' home and yet, here, she was looked down upon. She couldn't live with the contempt heaped upon her by her neighbors, by people like the Swans, the Murbacks . . ." She paused for a moment before she continued. "And the Casons."

"Revelation, I pass no judgment on you or your family," James said.

"Oh, but you do," Revelation said.

"How so?"

"I see it in your eyes every time you look at me. You think I'm a pretty woman, and you are a little flattered that I made a fool of myself, by throwing myself at you. But it is very obvious that, no matter how flattered, or interested, or intrigued you might be, you will never allow anything to develop between us, because you don't think I'm good enough for you."

"Now hold on, Revelation, I never said anything of the sort," James said. He put his hands, tenderly on her shoulders. "Actually, I think you are a rather uncommon woman, and I—"

"Uncommon," Revelation said, with a dismissive chortle. "Horned toads are uncommon creatures. You can't turn a woman's head using that kind of language."

"Revelation, please. You aren't being fair," James said.

Revelation's face softened. "I know I'm not. I shouldn't have thrown myself at you the way I did." She held up her right hand. "It was not very ladylike, and I'm sure you found it rather unsettling. I'll never do it again, I promise you. From now own I'll just be another one of the hands."

Revelation got to her feet and started up the side of the little knoll.

James waited until she was at the top of the hill before he called to her.

"Revelation?"

She turned to look back down at him. Again, her face was illuminated by the moon, so that her skin was a contrast in pearl and shadow. Maybe it was James's imagination but, at this moment, he didn't think he had ever seen anyone more beautiful, despite the men's clothing she was wearing.

"Maybe I don't want you to be just one of the hands."

"I'm sorry, James," Revelation said quietly. "It's too late for that now."

James watched as she disappeared down the other side of the little knoll. A moment later he heard the sound of hooves as she rode away. He turned, picked up a handful of small pebbles, then tossed them one by one into the water.

Revelation was right. He hadn't thought she was good enough for him. Until this moment, he hadn't realized what a snob he was. He vowed right there and then, to be less judgmental from now on. It was an epiphany.

Dakota Territory
Thursday, August 14, 1862:

Kris Dumey had enjoyed a good day in his diggings. Coming out of the tunnel he had dug into the side of the mountain, he was carrying a sack that was filled with gold nuggets. He had no idea how much it was worth, but his head was spinning with the excitement of it.

It was clear, now, that he was not going to be able to work his claim alone much longer. As he took out the last few nuggets, part of the wall collapsed, covering the area where he was working. At first he was going to dig it out again, then he decided to let the rocks stay where they were. There was no sense in making it too easy for someone else who might try and find his diggings.

Shadows fell across him as he emerged into the sunlight, and when he looked up, he saw six mounted men. Because the sun was behind them he saw them only in silhouette. Then one of the men spoke, and Kris felt a sense of foreboding, for he recognized the voice. The man who spoke was a dapperly dressed, handsome man, the self-appointed sheriff, Henry Plummer.

"Looks like you've had a little luck there, Dumey," Plummer said.

"Not much," Dumey replied, holding up the sack. "It's mostly just rocks," he said. "I thought I might get them out into the sunlight to see if there is any color."

"Well, what do you say we look at it together?" Plummer suggested. "Empty your sack."

Protectively, Dumey wrapped both arms around the sack.

"Whether I got any color or not, it ain't none of your business," Dumey said in protest.

"Of course it's my business," Plummer said. "I'm the sheriff, aren't I? And as sheriff, I am duly empowered to collect taxes."

"You aren't duly empowered to collect anything," Dumey insisted. "You aren't really the sheriff."

"Not yet," Plummer agreed. "But someone has to keep order around these parts until a real sheriff can be elected. I expect I will eventually be elected, so why not start serving the people now?"

"You're full of it, Plummer. You aren't serving anyone but yourself."

Plummer laughed. "Well, since the job isn't official, as yet, I have to pay myself and my deputies out of the taxes I raise from good people like you," he said.

"How much tax?" Dumey asked.

Plummer chuckled, then nodded toward the men who were riding with him. "Well, it takes a lot of money to run my office. As you can see, I have several fine deputies."

By now Dumey's eyes had adjusted to the bright sunlight, and he looked up at the men who were riding with Plummer.

"George Ives, I recognize. Them three I don't know." He pointed to the Butrum brothers. "But if they are like the other men you have riding with you, then you ain't got much."

"Sorry you don't like the quality of my help," Plummer replied. "But then, you don't have to like them. All you have to do is pay taxes."

Kris glanced over at his rifle. It was lying

against a rock, about thirty feet away. There was no way he could get to it in time, and, even if he could, it wouldn't do him any good. It was charged with only one shot, and there were six men facing him.

He sighed in defeat. "How much," he asked, reaching down into his sack.

"All of it," Plummer replied innocently.

"What? All of it? Are you crazy?"

"No," Plummer said. "I'm not crazy. I'm maybe just a little greedy. But I'm not crazy." He laughed, maniacally, then pulled the trigger, shooting Kris Dumey down in cold blood.

"One of you boys get the sack," he said. "We'll divide up the gold later."

Angus Butrum climbed down from his horse, took the sack from Dumey's dead fingers, then remounted.

"Take a look inside," Plummer ordered.

Angus stuck his hand down into the sack and pulled out a couple of rocks. Both rocks glittered with gold.

"Damn!" Angus said. "There's a fortune in this sack."

George Ives laughed. "I told you this was a sweet deal," he said. "Have you ever heard the term 'license to steal'? Well, my friend, that's what we've got. A license to steal."

Chapter Fifteen

*With the Golden Calf Cattle Company, mile 852
Thursday, August 14, 1862:*

As soon as he saw Revelation, James knew there
was something wrong. Her wagon was about a
mile ahead, sitting absolutely motionless. Slapping his legs against the side of his horse, he
urged the animal into a gallop, covering the mile
in just under three minutes.

When he reached the wagon, Revelation was
sitting quietly in her seat, holding the reins in
her hands, staring straight ahead.

"Revelation, what is it?" James asked. "Why
have you stopped?"

Revelation looked over at James. There was
an expression of shock and horror in her face.

"What is it?" James asked.

Without answering him, Revelation pointed
with a shaking hand.

Though it had been hidden by a small rise as

James approached the wagon, now he could see what had stopped Revelation in her tracks. There, just below the rise and not more than fifty yards away, was a burned-out wagon. But it wasn't the wagon that was holding her attention. It was what was lying on the ground alongside the wagon. There, naked and ghastly white, were three bodies. Each body was pierced by dozens of arrows, and from their scalped and broken heads, spilled brains lay in the dirt, cooked by the sun.

"Stay there," James said, swinging down from his horse.

"Don't worry," Revelation replied in a tight voice. "I'm not going anywhere."

James walked over for a closer look. It was a man and two women, though one of the women looked very young, perhaps in her teens. It was difficult to be certain, because the sun was already beginning to have its effect. At first, James thought the Indians had taken everything. Then he saw a small journal lying nearby, its leaves fluttering in the breeze.

James picked it up and began reading.

"What is it?" Revelation called. Though she hadn't come any closer, she had climbed down and was now standing alongside the wagon.

James walked back over to the wagon and showed Revelation the journal. She looked at it for a moment, then looked back toward the three bodies. Tears were streaking down her cheeks.

For the first time since leaving Bexar County, James saw a soft and vulnerable side to Revelation. He wasn't sure what made him do it, but he reached out to her, put his arms around her, and pulled her to him. She began to cry and he stood there for a long moment, not speaking, just holding her.

Finally Revelation was all cried out, and she pulled herself away from him then ran her hand through her hair, as if composing herself.

"I'm sorry," she said. "It's just such a sad thing to see. A family like that, excited by the future. Then, to have that future taken from them in such a horrible way."

"I know."

"What do we do now?" Revelation asked.

"I'm going to bury them," James said, removing a shovel from its straps on the side of the wagon. "Then we'll wait here for the others to catch up."

"What if the Indians are still here?"

James looked all around the area. "If they were still here, they would have shown themselves by now. I'd say that, for the present at least, we are safe."

"For the present," Revelation said.

"Yes."

"And what happens after the present?"

"We'll just have to cross that bridge when we come to it," James answered. He took the shovel back over to where the three bodies lay, covered by a swarm of flies. They were already a little ripe, so he moved upwind from them, then began to dig.

He was just patting down the dirt over the last grave when the others arrived. Seeing Revelation, James, and the burned-out wagon, Bob darted ahead of the herd, then rode quickly up.

"What is it? What happened here?"

"A man, woman, and their daughter were killed here," James explained. "I just buried them."

"Indians?"

"Yes."

"You think it was just a few renegades? Or are they on the warpath?"

"I don't know if they are on the warpath," James answered. "But from the number of arrows sticking out of everyone's body, I'd say that what was done here was done by more than just a few renegades."

By now Duke and Billy had joined them.

"A family, killed by Indians," Bob said, answering their unasked questions.

"So what do we do now? I mean, you aren't planning on turning back or anything like that, are you?" Bob asked.

"No way. We've come this far, we're going

the rest of the way. But we are going to have to be a little more careful."

"Careful how?"

"Well, for one thing, I don't plan to send Revelation ahead of us anymore," James said. "I think it will be safer for her if she stays back with us. Also, we had better keep our eyes peeled from now on. We may run across Indians, but I don't plan to be surprised by them."

Although it was more efficient for Revelation to travel ahead of the herd, set up camp, and have supper ready by the time the others arrived, she began traveling with the group. James's idea of having her stay back so she could travel with the rest of them made her feel a lot safer. Most agreed with James that this was the best thing to do, but the agreement wasn't unanimous. Matthew had argued against it yesterday, when James made the suggestion, and he had grumbled again this morning, just as they started out.

They had been underway for nearly an hour, when Matthew rode over to plead his case once more.

"Look here, Cason, keepin' Revelation back here with us ain't no good," he complained. "I mean, hell, drivin' cows is hard work. Whenever a man works that hard, he has a right to have him a hot meal ready and waitin' for him by the time he makes camp. And if'n Revelation don't go on ahead of us, why, it'll like as not be an hour, maybe two or three, before we get fed. They ain't nothin' right about that."

"Damn, Matthew, I would think you would have a little more consideration for the danger here," James said, shocked at Matthew's total lack of concern about Revelation's safety. "After all, it's your own sister we're talking about."

"Yeah, well, there's danger and then there's danger," Matthew said. "I've know'd Revelation a lot longer than you have, and believe me, I know she can take care of herself. Besides which, how do we know there are a lot of Indians out there. Far as we know, them people you found with arrows stickin' out of 'em, could've been killed by no more'n three or four Indians, out to rob 'em, or something."

"You could be right," James said. "Then again, you could be wrong. Take a look up there."

James pointed to a low-lying ridge of hills about three miles in front of them. Two twisted-rope columns of smoke climbed into the sky.

"What's that?" Matthew asked.

"Smoke signals," James replied.

Bob was riding about fifty yards away from where James and Matthew were having their conversation. When he also saw the smoke, he turned and rode back.

"You see the smoke?" he asked.

"I see it," James said.

"What do you think it means?" Bob asked.

"I figure these folks over here"—James pointed to the smoke on the right—"are inviting the folks over there"—he pointed to the smoke column on the left—"to dinner tonight. And they are plannin' on serving beef."

"Our beef?" Bob asked.

James shook his head. "Uh-huh, it looks that way."

"Well, hell, if that's all it is, maybe we ought to just give them some cows," Matthew suggested.

James shook his head. "No, we don't want to do that."

"Why not? You was awful damn quick to give them Indians down in the territories some of our cows. And that saloon keeper back at Fort Larned."

"That was different. We gave the saloon keeper a few cows to pay for the damage we did to his saloon. And down in the territories, you and your brothers violated their law, so we gave them cows in payment of a fine. It was a fair and equitable arrangement. If we were to give these Indians anything now, we would be surrendering to them. They understand weakness, so a few cows wouldn't be enough. They would want more and more until eventually they would want the entire herd."

"James's right," Bob said. "We can't give in to them."

"So, what are we going to do, fight the whole Indian nation?" Matthew asked. "There ain't but seven of us."

"There's eight of us," James said. "Don't forget Revelation. You just made a big point of telling me how she could defend herself, and I've seen enough of her to believe it."

"All right, eight of us. But that's against how many Indians? A thousand?"

"Could be a thousand, I suppose," James agreed. "Which means we'd better get ready for them." James put his fingers to his mouth, then gave a loud, piercing whistle. When the whistle got everyone's attention he made a circular motion over the top of his head, indicating that they should all gather around him.

Leaving the herd temporarily unwatched, everyone rode over to hear what James had to say.

"Bob, you are the best rider and you are well mounted," James said. "I want you to ride drag. Like as not the Indians will try and hit us from the rear."

"All right," Bob answered.

James held up his finger, then wagged it back and forth in admonishment. "But if you see them, don't try and fight them from back there.

What I want you to do, is hightail it on back up here and give us the warning."

"Right," Bob said.

"Billy, you'll be an outrider over on the left. Duke, you take the right. I'll take point."

"What about me 'n my brothers?" Matthew asked. "Where do you want us?"

"I want you boys to ride as close to the wagon as you can."

"I told you, Revelation can look out for herself," Luke said.

"It's not just Revelation I'm worried about. All our food is in that wagon. If we lose it, it's going be a long and hungry trip."

Matthew stroked his chin for a moment, then nodded. "Yeah," he said. "Yeah, I see what you mean."

"Let's get moving," James ordered.

The Indians hit in the middle of the afternoon on the next day. True to James's prediction, they tried to attack the herd from the rear.

Although Bob had been keeping his eyes open, it was difficult to maintain a constant vigil. As a result his first indication of the presence of Indians, was when an arrow whistled by him, then stuck in the ground a few yards ahead. Twisting in his saddle, he saw a large group of Indians, perhaps as many as twenty, riding toward him.

The Indians released a volley of arrows and

Bob watched in morbid fascination as a cloud of missiles climbed high into the sky, then whizzed down toward him. None of the arrows hit him, but some of the cattle bellowed in pain as the arrows stuck themselves in their flanks.

Remembering James's admonition not to try and fight the Indians but to bring warning, Bob slapped his legs against the sides of his horse, spurring it into a gallop. The horse took off like a cannonball, its hooves drumming into the dirt. James leaned forward, not only to urge greater speed from his horse, but also to present a smaller target to the Indians.

He could hear the animal breathing, feel the horse's muscles working as he galloped away from the Indians. He saw two more arrows fly by him.

"Indians! Indians!" he shouted.

Ahead of Bob, Duke Faglier was sitting calmly in his saddle, aiming his rifle back toward the Indians who were chasing Bob. Bob saw a flash of light, a puff of smoke, then the rifle's recoil before he heard the heavy roar of the discharge. He heard the ball whizzing past him and, curious, he turned to look over his shoulder. The head of one of the Indians seemed to burst open like a watermelon as the heavy ball crashed into it. A spray of red made a brief halo about the Indian's head, then he fell from his horse.

Other rifles roared as well, and Bob saw that

the Scattergoods were also firing. From ahead of him, James was riding hard to get back to join the fight.

Bob pulled up when he came alongside James, then he drew his own rifle from its saddle sheath and turned to face the Indians. He fired and had the satisfaction of seeing the Indian he aimed at go down.

James got another one, then Duke, his rifle reloaded, got his second.

The Indians were armed only with bows, and though they had the advantage of shooting arrows more rapidly than the muzzle-loading rifles could be fired, they didn't have the range.

Although the cattle didn't stampede, they did break into a run. That had its advantage and disadvantage. The advantage was that it forced the Indians to come to them, and it tended to keep them out of bow and arrow range while keeping them in rifle range. The disadvantage was that the wagon and the Scattergoods were very close to the edge of the herd, and should the herd stampede, the wagon might easily be overturned. That could be disastrous for Revelation. Concerned for her safety, James found himself looking toward the wagon as often as he was looking back at the Indians.

Some of the Indians pulled back from the pursuit and when he looked, James saw that they were gathering around a couple of cows that had been killed. That gave him an idea.

"Bob, Billy, shoot a cow!" James shouted.

"What?"

"Each of you shoot a cow! Duke, you keep doing what you are doing."

Bob, Billy, and James picked out a target on the outside of the running herd. All three fired at approximately the same time, and three animals went down. Nearly half the Indians still in pursuit broke off the chase to go to the slain cattle.

Duke killed another one of the Indians still in pursuit and one of the Scattergoods killed another. The remaining Indians suddenly found the odds no longer to their liking, and they turned back.

The herd continued to run, and by the time it slowed to a trot, then to a walk, the remaining Indians were at least two miles back on the prairie, small black forms bent over somewhat larger forms lying on the ground. It was obvious they were butchering the beef that had just fallen into their hands.

"Yahoo!" Bob said. "By God, we showed them a thing or two."

"I wonder how many of them we killed?" Billy asked.

"I think we got about eight of them," James

said. He looked over at Duke and smiled. "Half of them Duke got."

"I've never seen such shooting," Billy said. "Do all you boys up there in Missouri shoot like that?"

"We shoot a lot of squirrels," Duke said. "If you can hit a squirrel, you can hit an Indian. Indians are much larger targets."

The others were laughing as the Scattergoods finally worked their way out of the middle of the herd.

"What was you people doin' shooting our own cows like that?" Matthew asked angrily.

"It stopped the Indians," Bob replied.

"Me an' my two brothers was shootin' 'em down like we was killin' flies and I figured we 'bout had 'em stopped. Then the next thing I know, I see you fellas shootin' our own cows."

"Like I said, it stopped the Indians," Bob said again, more resolutely this time.

"Uh-huh. What it done was cost us a hundred and fifty dollars is what it done. And here after all the big talk about not givin' them any cows 'cause it would show weakness."

"We didn't give the cows to them," James explained. "They probably think that the cattle were killed accidentally. All they were interested in was a little beef, so I let them have some. But it came at a high enough cost to them, that I don't think we'll be seeing this bunch again."

James's assertion that they wouldn't be seeing that bunch again proved to be premature. The Indians returned again later in that same day, then again the next day, and the day following that.

While the Indians didn't attack in force—there were never more than a dozen or so with each attacking party—they did manage to make themselves bothersome. They were excellent horsemen, and they would ride in to bow and arrow range, clinging to the off-side of their horses, launching arrows from just above the backs of their mounts before making a hasty retreat.

While half the attacking party kept the cowboys busy, the other half would strike the herd. The braves would ride right up to the cows, keeping themselves mounted by squeezing their legs against the horses' backs. Then, as if they were hunting buffalo, they would shoot arrows into the cows, killing from eight to ten with each attack they launched.

Mile 1,110,
Sunday, August 31, 1862:

"Indians!" John shouted.

"Here come the heathen bastards again!" Luke added.

"All right, everyone get ready!" James said,

and rifles were cocked and brought into position to fire.

"Wait!" Duke shouted, holding up his hand. "Wait, don't shoot!"

"What do you mean don't shoot?" Matthew asked. "Look at 'em, all bunched up like that. Hell, we could kill half of 'em with one volley."

"No, wait," James said, lowering his rifle. "Duke is right. They aren't attacking."

"One of them is coming toward us," Bob said.

"Yes, but look, he's holding his lance over his head. I think he want to parley."

"I'll parley with the son of a bitch," Matthew said, taking aim. "I'm going to put a bullet right between that heathen's eyes."

"No, don't shoot!" James shouted.

Disregarding James's order, Matthew pulled the trigger. Even as he did so, however, Billy pulled his knife and placed his blade over the primer cap on Matthew's rifle. As a result, the hammer clicked harmlessly against the knife blade.

"What the hell?" Matthew said angrily. "What did you do that for?"

"So I didn't have to cut your throat," Billy answered. "Now, you put that rifle back in the sheath."

Grumbling, Matthew did as he was asked.

The approaching Indian had stopped when

Matthew gave every indication that he was about to shoot, but now he resumed riding, coming closer to them. When he reached them he stopped and held up his right hand, palm open, in a symbol of greeting.

"I am Washakie of the Shoshone," he said. "My people are at peace with the white man. I am a friend of the white man."

"A friend, huh? You sure haven't been acting like it these last few days," Matthew said.

"You have been doing battle with our enemy, the Sioux," Washakie said. He nodded. "You have fought the Sioux bravely and well, but you are safe now, for you are in Shoshone land. If the Sioux try to fight you again, we will protect you."

"What do you want for this protection?" James asked.

"Only that you be the friend of the Shoshone, as we will be your friend."

"And the gift of a few cows, I suppose?" Matthew asked, sarcastically.

"I have received many gifts, and I have given many gifts," Washakie said. "But my friendship does not depend upon gifts."

"Are you telling us you don't want any of our cows?"

"I want cattle, yes," Washakie replied. "But not as a gift. We wish to trade."

"What do you have to trade?" James asked.

Washakie looked at James, then the others who were with him.

"Soon it will be very cold. Do you have blankets and robes for the cold?"

"Damn!" James said. He looked at the others. "Damn, he's right! It was so hot when we left Texas that I never even thought about bringing something for the cold weather."

"If you do not have blankets and buffalo robes, you will freeze to death," Washakie cautioned.

"And you just happen to have those things that we need, right, Chief?" Matthew asked.

"We have such things, yes," Washakie replied.

"Well, you can just go peddle them somewhere else," Matthew said. "Because we ain't buyin'."

"Yes, we are buying," James said. "Unless you think you can keep warm up here just by putting on more than one shirt."

Chapter Sixteen

*With the Golden Calf Cattle Company, mile 1,560
Thursday, October 9, 1862:*

The day began with overcast skies and a northwest wind. Although it was tolerably warm in
the morning, the temperature started dropping
and by noon it was below freezing. Shortly after
noon the clouds delivered on their promise, and
a freezing rain began falling. Conditions went
from uncomfortable to downright miserable.
Sleet pummeled the riders and caused sheets of
ice build up, first on the horns of the cattle,
then on their coats and the coats of the horses.

Sheets of ice also built up on the buffalo robes
the riders were wearing. Ice crystals hung in the
mustaches and beards of the men, and on their
eyebrows. It even caused little icicles to hang
from the end of their noses.

Bob rode in advance of the herd, looking for
some place to shelter the animals. He came back

with the happy report that there was a canyon just a few miles ahead.

"What good will it do us? We'll never get them there," Billy shouted into the howling wind.

"We'll get them there. We've got to!" James shouted back. "If we don't, we are going to lose the entire herd. I didn't come this far to give up now!"

Billy's prediction that they wouldn't be able to get the herd into the shelter of the canyon came uncomfortably close to being true. The wind cut through man and beast like a razor-sharp knife, blowing sleet and freezing rain into the faces of the plodding cattle. The natural tendency was for the cows to turn around, presenting their tails to the wind, but if they did that, they would be going away from the canyon, so the cowboys worked hard to keep them going in the right direction. Making lashes of their lariats, they slapped the animals hard on the rump, forcing them to proceed into the face of the driving storm.

It was a long, hard drive until finally, just before nightfall, they entered the canyon. As they did so, the drive got easier, for the cattle, realizing now that the better choice for them was ahead, were anxious to get into the shelter.

The night that followed was bitterly cold, though they managed to push it back somewhat by building a large fire. Revelation got supper going. It consisted of biscuits and bacon, augmented by a big pot of coffee. The men, exhausted from the day's efforts, sat quietly, staring into the fire as they drank their coffee and ate their supper.

Then, Revelation surprised them with something else. She added sugar and cinnamon to the extra biscuit dough, formed the dough into little circles, and dropped them into a boiling pot of lard. Within minutes she was moving from cup to cup, pouring fresh coffee and passing out doughnuts. When she started, still one more time, to refill the cups, James called out to her.

"Here, Revelation," James said. "You don't have to do that. If we want more coffee, we can get our own."

"I don't mind," Revelation said. "I was warm and snug on the wagon seat today, while you men kept the herd moving."

Billy chuckled. "Warm and snug, huh? You looked like a big icicle when you climbed down from that seat. I don't know how you could call that warm and snug."

"Sit down, Sis. If anyone else wants coffee, I'll get it for 'em," Matthew said.

"Damn, Matthew, what's got into you?" Bob teased.

"I can be a good guy if I want to," Matthew

said. "It's just that most of the time, I don't want to," he added.

The others laughed.

Taking him at his word, Revelation hung the coffeepot from its hook over the fire, then sat down beside James.

"That was very nice of you, cooking sinkers for the men," James said, using the cowboy term for doughnuts.

"It was the least I could do for them. Everyone worked so hard today."

"Yeah, they did, didn't they?" James said. "They've endured a lot on this drive, but they've pulled together into a really great outfit."

"You've pulled them together," Revelation said.

"No, they pretty much did it themselves. I don't think there's anything one man could do with a group like this, if the men weren't willing to do it on their own."

"Still, they look up to you as their leader."

"I reckon," James said, clearly uncomfortable with the compliments.

"James, how much longer do you think this drive will last?" she asked.

"Well, if the map we got back at Fort Larned is accurate, I figure we've got about one more week. That is, if a blizzard doesn't come up and snow us in."

"Oh, do you think that will happen?" Revelation asked, anxiously.

"I hope not," James said. Then, when he saw that wasn't comforting enough to her, he added, "I don't think we're going to have to worry about a lot of snow, the sleet and freezing rain has pretty much taken about all this cloud has to offer."

"I hope you're right."

They were silent for a moment, then Revelation spoke again.

"After we get there and sell the cattle, how long will it be before the outfit starts back?"

"Well, the outfit won't go back," James said.

"What do you mean?"

"After we sell the herd, there won't be any more outfit. The Golden Calf Cattle Company will break up and everyone is going to be on their own," James said.

"What do you think they will all do?"

"I imagine everyone will hang around, at least through the winter, looking for gold."

"Oh, do you think so?"

"Well, yes. I mean, when you get right down to it, that's the real reason we came up here. The idea of the cattle drive came later."

"So, you're going to look for gold, too?"

"I may look for a little while," James answered. "Why are you so concerned? Are you that anxious to get back to Texas? Have you got someone waiting for you back there?"

"Someone?"

"A fella."

Revelation laughed. "No," she said. "Are you kidding? Who, in Bexar county, would be interested in a Scattergood?"

"I just wondered, I mean, with all the questions about how soon you could get back."

"I like to know what is going to happen next, that's all."

"Whether I find any gold or not, I don't plan to go back to Texas, to stay," James said. "I'll take Pa his share of the money from the sale of the herd, but then I'm coming back to Dakota."

"Why?"

"If Dakota is like California, even after the gold boom dies down, there will still be a lot of people up here. And if so, they'll have to eat. I plan to get myself as much grassland as I can and start a ranch."

"Yes," Revelation said. "Yes, I can see where that might be a good idea."

"I'm glad someone can see it. I've talked with some of the others about starting a ranch up here, and they don't seem to think it's a very good idea."

"So everyone else is going back?"

"I don't know what your brothers will do, but

Bob, Billy, and Duke plan to stay here, at least through the winter, to look for gold."

"I suspect my brothers have something like that in mind as well."

"What about you?"

"I suppose I'll have to stay for a while as well. I can't go back by myself."

James picked up a stick and tossed it into the fire, watching it catch in the flames. He looked over at Revelation. Her face glowed softly in the flickering light of the campfire. James cleared his throat.

"Revelation?"

"Yes?"

James was quiet for a moment.

"Yes?" Revelation said again.

"I've been watching you for this entire drive," James said. "You're strong, you're a hard worker, and you don't get rattled in danger. You're a good cook and you can make do without a whole lot of trappings. I mean, the sinkers you made for us tonight show that."

Revelation laughed. "Well, I thank you," she said. "I think."

James tossed another stick into the fire. "What I'm getting at is this. It's going to be a hard, lonely life starting a ranch up here. But I really feel like it could pay off in five or ten years. Now, those first few years would go down a heap easier if I had someone to share them with me. And, I expect there would be more reward in building a ranch, if I had a son to leave it to."

"I suppose so," Revelation said. She still wasn't certain she understood where James was going with this line of conversation.

"So, how about it?" he concluded.

"How about what?" Revelation asked, confused by the question.

"What's your answer? Yes or no?" James asked.

As Revelation realized what James was asking, she gasped.

"James Cason, are you proposing to me?"

"Proposing?"

"Are you asking me to marry you?"

"Well, yes," James said, as if surprised that she was just now figuring it out. "What do you think I've been doing?"

"Damn you, James," Revelation said.

"Damn me what?"

"Don't you know that a girl spends her entire life fantasizing about how she is going to be proposed to? She wants the moment to be romantic, she wants to be made love to, she doesn't want to think she's being hired as a ranch foreman."

"Oh," James said. "Well, I'm sorry. I didn't mean any offense."

"So ask me."

"What?"

"If you want me to marry you, James Cason, ask me the way a woman is supposed to be asked."

James was quiet for a long moment. Finally, he spoke.

"I'm not very good at this sort of thing, Revelation. I'm a plainspoken man, and I say what's on my mind. I always tell the truth about things, no matter which way it falls, so sometimes I get myself into a heap of trouble because I'm honest, when a little dishonesty would be a less hurtful thing.

"This, I will tell you true. I've been giving a lot of thought to starting a ranch up here, and almost from the beginning, I have known that I don't want to do this alone. And the more I thought about it, the more I realized that it's not just that I don't want to do it alone, I don't want to do it without you.

"You want me to ask you to marry me, the way a woman is supposed to be asked? Well, Revelation, I truly don't know how that is, so all I can do is tell you that I've been thinking about you a lot lately. And most of all, I'm thinking that I would like for you to be around from now on. I would like for us to share the rest of our lives together. So I'm asking you now, Revelation Scattergood, would you marry me?"

James had been staring into the fire for the whole time he was talking. When he looked back at Revelation he was surprised to see tears streaming down her face.

"Revelation, what's wrong? Have I upset you?"

"No, silly," Revelation said. "Don't you know that women also cry when they are happy?"

"You're happy?"

"Yes."

"Does that mean you'll marry me?"

"Yes," Revelation said, nodding her head vigorously. "I'll marry you, James Cason."

"Yahoo!" James shouted.

"What's got into him?" Matthew asked.

"I imagine your sister just told him she would marry him," Duke said.

"Well, it's about time," Matthew said. "She's been pining over him ever since we left Texas."

"Yeah, I figured it would've happened long before now," Billy said.

"I told you he wouldn't ask her until we were nearly through the drive," Bob said.

James listened to the exchange with an expression of surprise on his face. "Damn," he said. "Are you telling me everyone knew about this?"

Revelation laughed. "Everyone, it seems, but you," she replied, her eyes glistening happily in the firelight.

Chapter Seventeen

**With the Golden Calf Cattle Company, just
outside Bannack***
Wednesday, October 15, 1862:

Although they left Texas with 3,250 head of cattle, losses to Indians, accidents, weather, penal-
ties, and normal attrition, had cut down the size
of the herd. They wouldn't have a final count
until they drove the cows into the holding pens,
but they knew they were going to have to have
an equitable apportionment to share the losses.
After a great deal of discussion, James, Bob,
Billy, Duke, and the Scattergoods, came to a mu-
tual agreement as to how the loss would be ap-
portioned. James and Billy would take the
biggest loss, as they had left Texas with the
greatest number of cows. Bob and the Scat-

---

*Today, Bannack is a remarkably well-preserved ghost town, des-
ignated as a state park.

tergoods would take the second largest loss, while Duke, who had the fewest cows, would suffer the least loss.

That settled, they then authorized James to go into town to negotiate the best price he could get.

Leaving the herd in a grassy valley, James started into town to make arrangements to sell the cattle. He had ridden no more than two or three miles away from the cow camp when he saw them. Shielding his eyes against the bright blue sky, he looked at the circling birds about a mile away.

They were vultures, black messengers of death hanging on outstretched wings, waiting for their turn at some gruesome prize. James knew it would have to be something larger than a dead rabbit or a coyote to attract this much attention.

Curious as to what it might be, he continued riding toward the circling birds. It didn't take long to satisfy his curiosity. Just ahead, hanging from the straight branch of a big cottonwood tree, a corpse twisted slowly from the end of the rope. Even from where he was, James could hear the terrible creaking sound the rope was making.

"I don't know what you did, mister," James said quietly. "But whatever it was, you deserved better than this. Even the condemned aren't left hanging on the scaffold."

The corpse had an elongated neck, and its head was twisted and cocked to one side. The eyes were open and bulging and a blue, swollen tongue was sticking out of the corpse's mouth.

There was a sign on the tree, and James moved closer so he could read it.

ATTENTION:
THIS MAN STOLE MONEY. WE HUNG HIM FOR IT.
—THE BANNACK MINING DISTRICT VIGILANTES,
SHERIFF HENRY PLUMMER IN CHARGE.

James stood up in the stirrups so he could reach the rope around the man's neck. He opened his knife and began sawing at the rope, paying no attention to the two riders who were coming down the road from the direction of Bannack.

"Hold it there, mister!" one of the riders shouted. "Just what do you think you're doin'?" The rider was holding a rifle.

"What's it look like I'm doing?" James replied. He continued to saw at the rope. "I'm cutting this man down."

"Leave him be. Plummer wants him to hang there until he rots." The rider punctuated his statement by levering a cartridge into the chamber of his rifle. He raised the rifle to his shoulder, aiming it at James.

James sighed and sat back in the saddle. "Did you two do this?" he asked.

"We were part of it. We're deputies for Sheriff Plummer."

"What kind of court would sentence a man to hang for stealing? And what kind of sheriff would leave him hanging?"

The two men laughed.

"What's so funny?"

"There ain't no court, mister. There's only the sheriff."

"So in addition to being sheriff, this man Plummer is judge, jury, and hangman?"

"That's right."

"I can see right now it pays not to get into trouble around here."

The two men laughed. "Remember that, mister, and you might stay alive. Now, get on about your business and leave this be. This ain't none of your concern."

Nodding, James rode on toward town. He felt an itching in his back and knew that the rifle was still pointed at him. It took every ounce of strength to resist breaking into a gallop, but he was certain that if he did, the man with the rifle would shoot.

Bannack:

As 1862 began there was only a handful of white men, and almost no white women or children, in the area which had been, in succession, a part of the Louisiana, Missouri, then Dakota territories. Only later would it become Montana.

Few people had even heard the word Montana, and fewer still had any interest in the place until a man named John White discovered a rich placer deposit on Grasshopper Creek.

White wasn't the first to discover gold in Montana. There was some placer mining on Gold Creek near Hell's Gate (later renamed Missoula), where James and Granville Stuart had been panning gold earlier in the year. Then, M.H. Lott and his party discovered gold in the Big Hole River drainage, just over the hill from Grasshopper Creek.

Ironically, John White was looking for Lott when he stopped to pan dirt on the Grasshopper and made the biggest strike of all. It was his find that brought thousands of gold seekers from all over America. John White's discovery also led to the founding of the town of Bannack. Bannack would go on to become the first capital of the newly created territory of Montana.

When James rode into Bannack the first time, he saw a boomtown of over three thousand people, all of whom had been drawn by the hope of striking it rich. Not everyone who came to Bannack planned to get their gold out of the ground. Many came to make their fortune from those who got their gold by digging, thus the town was fully developed with saloons, restaurants, stores, and two hotels.

Unlike two decades earlier when it took treasure seekers from three to six months to reach the goldfields of California, Bannack could be reached by a combination of train, boat, and coach, in just over three weeks from almost any city in the East. That accessibility contributed to the boom and created a ready market for the Golden Calf Cattle Company's herd.

As soon as it was known that James was bringing in a herd of cattle to sell, he had three contractors bidding for his business. The only disappointment was the fact that the cows brought a little less than he had thought. He left Texas thinking he could make fifty dollars a head, but the offers ranged from twenty-nine to thirty-seven dollars.

James sold for thirty-four dollars a head. That wasn't the highest offer, but it was an offer of cash, whereas the others wanted to pay by bank draft, redeemable in St. Louis. James had no intention of going to St. Louis for his money.

Returning to the herd, James told the others what he had learned, and explained the deal he had made.

"I think you shoulda taken the thirty-seven dollars," Luke Scattergood said. "I mean, thirty-seven dollars is better than thirty-four. Even I know that."

"Yes, but if we take the thirty-four dollars, we can leave here with cash in hand," James said. "The other deal would require us to go to St. Louis for the money. If the money was really there, and if we could get there. Don't forget, there is a war going on."

"I think you did the right thing," Bob said. Billy quickly agreed, as did Duke.

"I think it was the right thing as well," Revelation said.

"Well, of course you would think that. You're stuck on him," Luke said.

"But she's right," Matthew said. "Cash in hand is better than a bank draft in some far-off place."

Reluctantly, Luke accepted the fact that the deal was made.

Everyone turned out to watch as James and the others drove their herd down Main Street to the cattle pens at the other end of town. There was excitement in the air, as people contemplated adding roast beef and beefsteak to what had become a monotonous menu of pork, chicken, and wild game. The townspeople were also fascinated with the idea that this herd had been driven all the way up from Texas, along the Bozeman Trail, right through the heart of hostile Indian territory.

As the cattle were driven into the pens, Milton Poindexter, the contractor who bought the herd, and James kept a head count. They did this by putting a knot in a strip of rawhide for every tenth cow. There were several rawhide strips, and each strip had ten knots. The final tally was 2,976 head. After the count was made, Poindexter went to the bank with James to withdraw the money.

"The current price of gold is fifty dollars an ounce," the banker explained to James. "You can accept payment in gold or specie."

"Specie?"

"Paper money," the banker said. "Government greenbacks. If I were you, I would take it in specie, as it will be much easier to handle than gold."

James thought about it for a moment. Greenbacks would be easier, but given the volatility of the war, and the fact that all Union money in Texas had been exchanged for Confederate dollars, he decided the most stable currency would be gold.

"I think I'll take it in gold."

"Very well, sir. It'll take a few moments to weigh and fill your sacks."

The banker began weighing gold dust, then

pouring the measured dust into sacks, each sack containing one hundred ounces.

"That's a lot of gold dust," James said, looking at the sacks that were beginning to stack up.

"It's going to come to 125 pounds," the banker said. "Gold dust is heavy."

"Yes, I know it is."

The banker chuckled. "That's probably a pretty good thing, though. Most robbers steal because they are too lazy to work. But if a robber takes gold he is going to have to work because it is so heavy. Still, there is always that chance," the banker said. "That being the case, you might want to leave it on deposit with the bank."

"Perhaps I will," James said. "But first I need to take it to my partners so we can divide it up."

As the banker continued to fill the sacks, James walked over to talk to Poindexter.

"As I was coming into town, I saw a man hanging from a tree," James said. "I started to cut him down, but two men stopped me."

James thought he saw an expression of fear dart across the contractor's face. Poindexter's eyes narrowed, and he nervously ran his hand through his hair, but he said nothing.

"You wouldn't happen to know who it was, would you?"

"Who?"

"The dead man I just told you about. Do you know who it was?"

"His name was Gillis. Logan Gillis," Poindexter said.

"Well, Logan Gillis paid dearly for stealing. Normally I don't have any sympathy for a thief, but I figure he deserved better than that."

"Gillis wasn't a thief," Poindexter said.

"That's what the sign said."

"Our—*sheriff*—left that sign," Poindexter said, slurring the word sheriff.

"Henry Plummer?"

Again, Poindexter looked nervous. "Do you know Henry Plummer?"

"No. But the sign bore his name. Also the two men who stopped me said they were deputies."

The beef contractor made a scoffing sound. "Those men aren't deputies, because Plummer is no more a sheriff than I am. He sure would like to be sheriff, though. And he has started a vigilante committee to protect the good people of the Bannack Mining District. But he's the one we need protecting from. Look at Logan Gillis. If the truth were known, Plummer and his men probably stole money from Gillis, then hung him for trying to keep hold of his own."

"Does everyone feel the same way about Plummer?" James asked.

"Everyone who isn't on his payroll feels that

way about him. But he has so many men working for him as deputies, and so many others frightened, that if we were to hold a real election today, he would win."

"Sounds to me like he's the kind of person a fella wants to stay away from," James said.

"You've got that right, mister."

It was the last building on the street, sitting just on the edge of the town. The sign in front read SHERIFF'S OFFICE, BANNACK MINING DISTRICT VIGILANTE COMMITTEE, HENRY PLUMMER, SHERIFF.

A woodfire popped and snapped inside a small, potbellied stove, warming the inside of the building. Half a dozen men stood around the stove and around the single desk that occupied the room. Henry Plummer sat in a swivel chair with his feet propped up on the desk. He was buffing to an even higher shine his already polished boots.

"That was quite a show this morning, all those cows coming through," Plummer said as he worked the shoe brush back and forth over the burnished leather. He looked up at Angus. "Is this is the herd you've been waiting for?"

"Yes," Butrum replied.

"Well, I congratulate you, Mr. Butrum. It was worth waiting for. They were paid over a hundred thousand dollars for the herd, all in gold," Plummer said. He put the brush back in the desk drawer then admired the sheen on his shoes. Looking up at the others, he smiled. "Yes, sir, it's going to be a very good payday."

"Wish he'd taken the money in paper, it would'a been a lot easier," George Ives said.

"Ives, I swear, you would complain if they hung you with a new rope," Plummer said. "If the gold is too heavy for you, I'm sure some of the others will be glad to take your share."

"No, no, it's not too much for me."

Plummer laughed. "I didn't think it would be."

"When are we going to do it?"

"As soon as I figure out the best way to do it," Plummer answered. "Probably some time tomorrow."

"What about Faglier?" Angus asked.

"Who's Faglier?" Plummer replied.

"I told you who he is. He's the one me an' my brothers been lookin' for all this time. He's one of the cowboys that brought the herd up."

"Do you know which one he is?"

"Yeah, one of the men down at the holding pens pointed him out today. We know him, but he don't know us."

"Well, that ought to make it easy enough for you tomorrow."

"We don't aim to wait until tomorrow to give him a chance to get away," Percy said.

"We're going to kill him today."

"No, you aren't. You are going to wait until tomorrow," Plummer said, scowling at the three brothers. "I don't intend to let that money get away from me because you have some score to settle."

"All right, we'll do it your way. If you want us to wait, we'll wait," Angus said. "As long as you know we intend to kill him."

"You can kill him," Plummer said easily. "It doesn't make any difference to me. All I'm interested in is the money."

Chapter Eighteen

Former cow camp outside Bannack, Dakota Territory,
Thursday, October 16, 1862:

Duke Faglier poured a little gold dust into his hand, examined it for a moment, then returned it to the sack. "Seventy-five hundred dollars," he said. "I've never held so much money in my hand at one time in my life." He chuckled. "In fact, I don't think all the money I've ever handled would equal this."

"What are you going to do with all that money, Duke?" John asked.

"I don't know yet, but I figure I'll find some way to spend it."

"What about a saloon?"

Duke chuckled. "Well, I might buy a few drinks, but I don't know as I want to spend it all in a saloon."

"Not *in* a saloon, *for* a saloon," John said. "Me an' Luke are goin' to spend the winter lookin' for gold. But come next spring, we're thinkin' on buyin' us a saloon. We figure, with all the gold money up here, a saloon would do real well. Maybe you'd like to come in as our partner."

"Well, I don't know," Duke answered. "I don't know, let me think about that."

"I'll tell you what I'm going to do," Billy said. "Well, after I poke around in the hills a while, I guess I'll take my uncle's money back to Texas. Then I'm going out to California."

"California," Matthew said. "Now, there's an idea. I've always had a hankering to see that place myself."

"That leaves you, Bob. What are you going to do?" James asked.

"You won't care much for what I have in mind," Bob replied.

"What do you mean?"

"I aim to get into the war," Bob said. "I thought about it a lot during the drive up here. I'm not sure I understand all the reasons why the war come about, but I know I won't be able to hold my head up if I don't get into it."

"So, come next spring, you'll be going back to Texas?"

Bob shook his head. "No, I'm going now.

253

They say the boats will be running for about another month until river ice shuts them down. I'm going with the next boat."

"You mean you ain't goin' to look for gold?" Luke asked. "I thought that was the whole reason you come up here."

"It was," Bob said. "But I've changed my mind. I feel like I have to go back."

"Well, it's your decision, Bob," James said. "A man has to do what a man has to do. I wish you luck."

"Thanks."

"Now, I have a proposal," James said.

"What's that?" Billy asked.

"I propose that we all go into town and spend tonight in the hotel. It might be nice to have a roof over our heads for a change."

"Yeah, and no cows bellowing," Luke said.

"Or wandering off," Bob suggested.

"Or stinking," Billy added. The others laughed.

Bannack, two a.m.
Friday, October 17, 1862:

Percy tripped as he stepped up onto the boardwalk in front of the Last Chance Saloon, across the street from the Miner's Hotel.

"Shhh!" Chance whispered. "You're making enough noise to wake the dead."

"I didn't see the step in the dark."

"Well, hell, it ain't like they just put it there," Chance said. "It's been right there as long as we've been here."

"Will both of you shut up?" Angus ordered.

Percy and Chance stopped their arguing as the three men moved to the edge of the boardwalk. At this time of night, the town was absolutely quiet, the last customer from the last saloon having left nearly two hours earlier.

Except for the hotel, every building in town was dark. There, a lamp in the lobby downstairs, and another in the hallway upstairs provided the only sign of illumination in the entire town.

"Plummer isn't going to like it when he finds out that we didn't wait to kill Faglier," Percy said.

Angus chuckled. "Yeah, well, he's going to like it even less when he finds out that we took the money."

"You really think we should take the money, Angus?" Chance asked. "What about Plummer and The Innocents?*

"To hell with Plummer and The Innocents. The way I figure it, this has been our deal from the start. We're the ones that found out about the herd, and the whole reason we come up here was to take the money. Maybe you boys would like to give Plummer some of your share of the

*"I am innocent," was the password of Plummer's gang, thus their name, The Innocents.

money, but I don't intend to give him any of mine."

"I ain't goin' to give them any of my money," Percy said.

"Me, neither," Chance added.

"All right, let's do it, then."

The three men moved out of the shadow of the saloon, were visible in the relative brightness of the moon-splashed street, then disappeared once more in the shadows of the buildings on the other side. Angus pulled his pistol and the others did the same.

"Check your loads," he said.

All three men spun the cylinders, checking that all chambers were charged. Then, with guns drawn, and moving quietly, they stepped into the hotel.

The hotel clerk was snoring loudly, asleep on a small cot behind the desk. Angus walked over to the counter and turned the registration book around to look at it. In the light of the desk lamp, he found what he was looking for.

"Duke Faglier, room 107," he whispered. "Get the key."

Reaching behind the counter, Chance got the key for 107.

"We'll take care of Faglier first," Angus whispered, indicating that they should go up the stairs.

"What about the keys to the other rooms?" John asked.

"We won't need them," Angus answered. "When we open the ball with Faglier, the others are going to come running out of their rooms to see what's going on. They'll be confused and muddled. We can shoot them down like ducks in a pond."

Quietly, the three men climbed the stairs. When they reached the top of the stairs they looked down the long hallway, which was dimly illuminated by one flickering lantern.

Tiptoeing quietly down the hallway, they came to room 107. Pausing at the door they listened, hearing the sound of snoring coming from inside. Angus slipped the key in the lock, then turned it slowly. Once the door was unlocked, he twisted the knob, then pushed the door open.

A wide bar of pale yellow light from the hall splashed into the room, dimly illuminating a sleeping figure on the bed. The three men raised their pistols, pointed at the sleeping figure, then, at a nod from Angus, began shooting.

James was startled from sleep by the sound of gunfire. Pulling his pistol from the holster that hung at the head of the bed, he rolled out of bed and onto the floor, then crawled to the door. Opening the door, he saw, in the light of the hall lamp, three men, backing out of Duke's room, firing back into the room as they did so.

Another door opened between James and the three shooters, and James saw a muzzle flash as that person began firing.

"We're sitting ducks!" one of the shooters shouted. "Get that lamp out!"

One of the other shooters began firing at the lamp.

"Not that way, you fool!"

The lamp exploded with a shower of glass and a spray of kerosene. The kerosene splashed onto the wall, then caught fire.

"Revelation!" James shouted. Standing up, he ran out into the hall, exchanging fire with the three shooters. Muzzle blasts, like flashes of lightning, lit up the hall.

"James!" Revelation shouted from behind one of the doors.

"I'm coming in," James shouted. James smashed through the door with his shoulder. Revelation was kneeling behind the bed, with her rifle pointed toward the door.

James saw Revelation fire and he leaped to one side. "No, it's me!" he shouted. Almost before he got the words out of his mouth, however, a body fell inside the room from behind him. One of the shooters had followed him into the room, only to be shot down by Revelation.

James went back to the open doorway and,

looking down the hall, saw Duke come out of one of the rooms.

"Faglier!" one of the two remaining shooters shouted. "It can't be! We killed you!"

James had never seen anything like what happened next. Without flinching, or ducking into any of the rooms, or even turning sideways to offer a smaller target, Duke faced the two men. Standing in the middle of the hall, he exchanged gunfire with the two shooters. The hallway was rapidly filling with smoke, both from the many pistol discharges as well from the fire that was rapidly investing the entire floor. The smoke was so thick now that the only thing that could be seen were the muzzle flashes from repeated firing.

Then the flashes stopped and the hallway fell silent, except for the snapping and popping of burning wood.

"I think they're down," Duke said. "Everyone, out of your rooms. Get out of the hotel, fast! It's on fire!"

Now all up and down the hallway, doors opened as guests who had been hiding from the gun battle appeared. In nightgowns and nightshirts, and coughing against the smoke, they found their way out into the hall.

"Hurry, hurry!" Duke shouted, as he directed the traffic. Billy, Bob, Luke, and John joined the guests as they all started toward the head of the stairs where, mercifully, the smoke wasn't quite as thick. James and Revelation came out into the hall as well.

"Where's Matthew?" Revelation shouted.

"He won't be coming," Duke said, waving toward the head of the stairs with his pistol. "Come on, hurry, we've got to get out of here or we'll be smothered by the smoke!"

"Where is he?" Revelation asked again.

"He was the first one to get shot," Duke said.

"Then he's wounded, we've got to go to him. We've got to help him!"

"Revelation, listen to me!" Duke shouted, putting his hands on her shoulders. "He's dead! There's nothing we can do for him now. We've got to get out of here or we're going to die, too!"

By now it was practically impossible to breathe, and all three were coughing at every breath.

"Get down on the floor!" James shouted. "It won't be as thick down there!"

All three dropped to the floor, then crawled to the stairs. When they reached the top of the stairs they launched themselves down, rolling and sliding until they reached the bottom. By now, the lobby was filled with smoke as well and, just as they started toward the main door, part of the ceiling fell in, blocking, with flaming refuse, their only escape route.

"We're trapped!" Revelation shouted.

In the wavering light of the fire that was consuming the hotel, James saw the lobby hall tree. Picking it up, he tossed it through the window, smashing out the glass.

"Get out through the window," James shouted over the now roaring flames. "But be careful of the shards."

James and Duke lifted Revelation through the window. Duke was next, followed by James. Outside the burning hotel, they regained their feet, then, coughing and wheezing, hurried across the street to join the crowd of hotel guests who were watching in horror as the building they had just exited was going up in flames.

By now several of the town's citizens, awakened by all the noise, had joined the guests.

"Form a bucket brigade!" someone shouted. "We've got to save the buildings next door!"

Within minutes, dozens of buckets appeared. A line was formed from a nearby watering trough and, while two men pumped water into the trough to keep the level high, others dipped buckets of water out, passing the filled containers from hand to hand down the line of volunteers toward the fire. They wasted no water by throwing it onto the fire itself; it was already too late for that. Instead, they concentrated on the adjacent buildings in the hope they could prevent them from catching.

Bannack Cemetery
Sunday, October 18, 1862:

They buried Matthew Scattergood and the three Butrum brothers in the same cemetery. The Butrums had been buried the day before with nobody but the gravedigger present as the three hastily built pine boxes were lowered into the ground.

Several of the citizens of the town turned out for Matthew's burial, including Milton Poindexter, the broker who had bought the herd, and Ethan Ellis, the banker. Matthew even had a preacher read over him as the beautiful black and silver casket was lowered.

"Poor Matthew," Duke said. "He wanted a room next to the street, so we changed rooms. If we hadn't done that, he would be alive now."

"And you would be dead," James said.

"Maybe. But at least the Butrums had some call to want to kill me. They had no call at all to shoot Matthew."

"Sure they did," Bob said. "They had the same reason to shoot him that they had to shoot all of us. They wanted our money."

"I'm convinced that Henry Plummer and his bunch wanted it as well," James said. "So if you think about it, the Butrums probably did us a favor. They weren't able to pull off the robbery by themselves. If they had waited, if Plummer and his entire gang had come after us, we might all be lying there."

"Maybe so, but at least they wouldn't have gotten the money," Duke said. "It was smart of you to suggest that we leave it in the bank."

"Yes," Bob said. "And I, for one, intend to leave it there, every cent of it, until I head back to Texas."

"You can't leave every cent there. You're going to have to take some of it out," James said.

"Why is that?"

"You'll need to buy a suit for the wedding."

Chapter Nineteen

*North Shadows Ranch on Beaverhead River
in the newly created territory of Montana
Sunday, January 10, 1864:*

After a winter of looking for gold with only lim-
ited success, James went south to Texas. He
stayed there just long enough to introduce his
new bride, and give his father his share of the
money from the sale of the herd. Then he returned to Bannack, staked out some land in a
grassy valley near Beaverhead River, and established North Shadows Ranch.

For now, North Shadows Ranch was much
more about land than it was about cattle. That
was because he had only a couple of seed bulls
and a dozen or so heifers. However, there was
plenty of water and grass, as well as sheltering
canyons against the cold Montana winters, so

James was totally convinced that his venture would eventually pay off.

Duke, Luke, and John had not even returned to Texas, but stayed in Bannack to open the Lucky Strike Saloon. Their endeavor proved to be extremely successful, for within less than a year, the Lucky Strike was the largest and finest saloon between Chicago and San Francisco.

Revelation didn't go with James when he went into town to go to church on the morning of January 10, 1864. She stayed home because the baby, Matthew Garrison, was sick.

James's first stop was the post office, where he checked his box. Along with his mail was a small sheet of paper with the numbers 3-7-77 on it. Those were the numbers used by the Montana Vigilante Association. The numbers referred to a grave: three feet wide, seven feet deep, and seventy-seven inches long. To the lawless, those numbers meant terror. To the lawful, they were a signal that an important event was about to take place.

After leaving the post office, James went to the apothecary. Sam Atkinson, the druggist who lived in an apartment upstairs over his store, was just coming down the outside stairs when James got there.

" 'Morning, James," Sam greeted. "Going to church?"

"I am, but I need something. Sam, before you go to church, would you open up your store long enough to sell me some medicine for little Matthew? He's feeling poorly."

"Of course I will," Sam replied. "Come on inside."

James watched as Sam used the mortar and pestle to grind a couple of powders into a single potion.

"Did you get one of these?" James asked quietly, showing Sam the paper with the numbers 3-7-77.

Sam looked at the paper, then glanced around before he answered.

"Yes, I got one," he answered, just as quietly.

"Do you know what it's about?"

"Last night Nelson Story and the vigilantes arrested Henry Plummer and some of his men. Milton Poindexter wants to hold a miners' court. If you got one of those, that means he plans for you to be on the jury."

"When is the trial?"

"This morning, right after church," Sam said.

"Well, if I'm going to make the trial, then I better not go to church. I need to get this medicine back to Revelation."

Sam poured the concoction into an envelope and gave it to James. "Twenty-five cents," he said. "Have your wife mix about a quarter of a spoonful of the powder with three-fourths of a

266

spoon of water. Give him one dose, three times a day. That should take care of it."

"Thanks," James said. "Oh, and if you see Poindexter, tell him I'll be back as soon as I can."

"Go to the Lucky Strike Saloon. That's where we are going to have the trial," Sam said.

Revelation was sitting in a rocking chair, holding the baby when James got home.

"How is Matthew?" James asked.

"I think he's feeling better some," Revelation said. "He's not as fussy as he was."

"I got the medicine for him," James said. "Sam says you can give him three doses a day. I also picked up the mail."

"Mail, oh wonderful," Revelation said. "Sit down, we'll read it together."

James shook his head. "I'll have to read it later," he said. "There are big doings going on in town."

"Oh? What?"

"Story has arrested Plummer and some of his men. They're going to try him today, and they want me to sit on the jury."

"It's about time justice caught up with that man," Revelation said. "Remember everything that happens at the trial, so you can tell me all about it."

"I will," James promised as he left.

Revelation put the mail on the kitchen table,

planning to wait until James returned to read the mail. But as she went about her chores, her eyes kept darting over to the envelopes, pregnant with the promise of news from home. Finally, she couldn't hold off any longer, so she picked up the mail, moved a chair to the window for its light, then opened one of the envelopes.

The first letter was from Billy Swan, who was now living in San Francisco, California. Billy had thrilling news in his opening sentence.

I'll bet you thought no woman would ever want me, but I am getting married.

I intend to bring her to Bannack to meet all of you as soon as possible. I can't wait for you to meet her. She is a wonderful girl and, Revelation, I've told her all about you, and how marvelous you were on that long cattle drive. She is very eager to meet you, and I know the two of you will get on well.

At the end of the letter, Billy asked them to take his letter to Duke, Luke, and John.

Since they are running a saloon right there in Bannack it will be easy for you to give them this letter. That way I won't have to write again. You know how bad I am about writing, it was hard enough to write this one letter, let alone another.

Feeling very good about that letter, Revelation put it aside for James to read when he came home, then she picked up the next one. It was from Bob Ferguson. True to his promise, Bob had joined the Confederate army shortly after he returned to Texas. Because of that, he couldn't send mail directly to Bannack but had to forward his mail through his parents, back in Texas. As a result, the letter made such a circuitous route that it was over four months old.

I have been made an officer. Can you see me as an officer? I told the captain that the Confederacy must really be scraping the bottom of the barrel if they can make an officer out of the likes of someone like me.

"I think you will be a fine officer," Revelation said aloud.

Even though I am now an officer, I don't like the army anymore than I did when I was a private. I should have listened to you, James. This war makes no sense. Good men are killing good men for no good reason that I can see.

I just wish the whole thing was over. But I have a plan. I intend to just keep getting promoted until I am a general. Then, when I'm a general, I'll tell all the men to go home, and the war will be over. What do you think about that as an idea?

Revelation laughed out loud at that suggestion.

Sometimes when we are in camp and the nights grow long, I think back to the cattle drive we made, and I recall every moment of it with fondness. James, before I left for the army, you asked if I would be interested in coming back to Bannack when the war is over, and ranching with you. I didn't give you an answer then, but I give you one now.

Yes, I would love to come up there and be your foreman, as my father was foreman for your father. That thought, and that thought alone, sustains me through this awful war.

Just as Revelation finished Bob's letter, the baby coughed. She put the letter down, then gave the baby his first dose of medicine. After that, she made certain he was covered up, then she sat back down to read the last letter. This one was from James's parents, but as it was addressed to both of them, she felt no compunctions about reading it.

She began crying from the very first paragraph.

We have some very sad news to report. Bob Ferguson was killed on October 25 at Pine Bluff, Arkansas. It wasn't much of a battle—it didn't even make the news here—but it was devastating as far as our county is concerned. Bob wasn't the only one killed. You remember young Carl Adams, who used to ride for us? He was killed as well.

Abner Murback, Syl Largent, and Joe Baker were killed earlier in the year. This war has not been kind to Bexar boys. I am so glad you did not go. And I so wish you had been able to keep Bob with you. As you can well imagine, Dusty and Betty Ferguson are having a very hard time with it. We are, too. Bob was like a second son to us, and the brother that you never had.

At that moment, James was blissfully unaware of the fate of his longtime friend. He was in the Lucky Strike Saloon, visiting with Duke, Luke, and John, waiting for the trial to begin.

"This is where the trial is to be, isn't it?" James asked, checking the clock on the wall behind the bar.

271

"That's what Dimsdale* has been telling everyone," Duke said.

"Here comes Poindexter now," Luke said. "Let's see what he has to say."

Poindexter stepped just inside the door and motioned to everyone. "If you fellas want to see the hanging, you'd better come on. They're fixin' to do it right now."

"What? They are hanging him already?" James asked. "Where was the trial?"

"There was no trial," Poindexter said. "There isn't going to be one."

James shook his head. "This is not good," he said. "There should be a trial."

"Why?" Luke asked. "Folks say Plummer is responsible for more than one hundred killings. If ever anyone needed hangin', it is Henry Plummer."

"Folks aren't saying that," Duke replied. "Dimsdale is saying that. He's been firing up people with those articles he's written. He's the one that's pushed it to this point."

"You ain't saying Plummer doesn't deserve to hang, are you?" John asked.

"No, I'm not saying that," Duke said. "I'm just saying that if we hang him without a trial, it's going to come back to haunt us some day."

"How?"

*Thomas J. Dimsdale, an Englishman, was editor of the Bannack newspaper.

"Duke is right," James said. "This could cause us trouble. We've just become a territory and I'd like to think we might be a state someday. But who is going to want us to be a state with lynching going on?"

"It's not a lynching exactly," Poindexter said. "It's more like a hanging."

"It's a hanging without a trial," James said. "In my book, that's a lynching."

"There are about three hundred people down there at the gallows," Poindexter said. "Do you want to try and stop them?"

"I would if I could," James said.

"Well, are you going to come down there? Or are you just going to stay here and talk about it?" Poindexter asked.

James, Duke, Luke, and John followed Poindexter down to the far end of the street, where several of the townspeople were gathered around the gallows. Ironically, the gallows had been built by Henry Plummer. Plummer, and two of his henchmen, were standing alongside the scaffolding. All three men had their hands tied behind them.

"Before we send these three scoundrels to their Maker, is there anyone who wants to speak for them?" Captain Nelson Story asked.

"I will speak for them," James said, hurrying toward the crowd.

"Bless you, James," Plummer said quickly. "I

always knew you were a decent sort. And I know that you know that I am innocent of any wrongdoing."

James shook his head. "I don't know that you are innocent, Plummer," he said. "In fact, I am certain that you are guilty, and you have blasphemed the very concept of innocence by using that as the password for your crimes."

"Well, if you know he's guilty, what are you speakin' for him for?" someone asked from the crowd.

"I'm not speaking for him as much as I am speaking for us. All of us," James replied. "If we hang these men without a trial, we are as guilty of murder as we believe them to be. We are never going to get law and order here unless we are lawful and orderly ourselves."

"What do you propose we do with him? Slap him on the wrist and tell him not to do it again?"

"I propose we hold a trial."

"Mr. Cason, I appreciate what you are trying to do," Captain Story said. "But think about this. If we had a trial, by jury, the jury would have to come from among our own number. Isn't that right?"

"Yes."

"That means that we would select a jury from right here. Do you really think there are twelve men here who would say Plummer is not guilty?"

"Hell no!" several from the crowd shouted.

"Do you think there are six men? Three? Two?" Story asked. "If you can find one man in this crowd, who would vote against hanging these outlaws, I would consider waiting."

James looked into the faces of all those present. It was obvious by their expressions that not one among their number would vote for leniency for Plummer or the two men who stood with him.

"I don't think I could find one man," James said.

"I don't think so, either," Story said. "That means that for all practical purposes we have just had his trial, haven't we?" Story turned to the crowd. "Gentlemen of the jury, how say you?"

"Guilty!" they shouted as one.

"So say you one, so say you all?"

"Guilty!" they shouted again.

Story turned to Plummer. "All right, Plummer, you heard the verdict. Get up there."

"No," Plummer said. "Story, you can't do this. You've got no right to do this."

"Wait!" one of the miners shouted. When the others looked at him, he said, "Hang Plummer's two pards first. I want Plummer to watch it, so he'll know what's going to happen to him."

"Yes!" several others agreed.

"All right. We'll hang the others first," Story agreed.

James stood in the crowd, feeling uneasy about what he was seeing but knowing that there was nothing he could do about it, and also knowing that, though technically wrong, justice was being served.

Plummer's henchmen went to the gallows, one at a time. Though both were offered a chance to say their last words, neither accepted the offer. James had to give them credit for facing the end stoically.

Now it was time for Plummer, and Plummer looked over at the ground behind the gallows where lay the bodies of two men who, but moments earlier, had been living creatures. Plummer began to shake uncontrollably.

"No," he said. He sunk to his knees. "No, please! I beg of you! I don't want to die! Cut off my finger, my hand, a foot! But spare me! Let me live! Please, have mercy!"

"Like you had mercy on over one hundred men?" Story replied. "Henry Plummer, you have killed many a man for their money, and every man you killed was a better man than you."

Captain Story nodded at the hangman, and

the hangman slipped the noose around Plummer's neck.

At that moment, Plummer seemed to find some modicum of courage. He quit begging, pulled himself together, and looked straight ahead. "All right, boys, if you are going to do this, give me a good drop," he said.

Plummer was pushed off the stand. He dropped quickly, was brought up short at the end of the rope, then twisted slowly in a quarter turn to the left.

James intended to tell Revelation about the day's events as soon as he returned home. Before he could do so, however, she told him about Bob being killed.

"He's been dead for nearly three months," she said. "All this time we thought he was alive, but he wasn't. He was dead while I was reading the letter from him, but I didn't know that. Somehow, that doesn't seem right."

Although she had cried when she read the letter, she cried again now as she told James about it, and James held her in his arms until she was all cried out. He let her cry for as long as she wanted, making no effort to stop her. In his mind he replayed moments from his lifelong friendship with Bob, the times they fished, hunted, and wrestled together. He could always beat him in running. James held Revelation close to him and felt her tears on his own cheeks and wished that it would be all right for him to cry as well.

It was threatening snow by the time night fell, so James carried in an extra measure of firewood. After dark, the clouds delivered on their promise and snow drifted down from the heavens, covering North Shadows in a mantle of white. James banked the fire, then they went to bed. Revelation lay beside him with her head on his shoulder and James told her that it was all over.

"What?" she asked. "What is all over?"

"The thieving, rustling, and murdering that's been going on around here. It's all over. Henry Plummer and his entire gang have been rounded up."

"What are they going to do with him?"

"They've already done it," James answered. "They hung Plummer and two of his men today, and I imagine they'll hang the rest of them over the next few days. No trial, they just hung them. I don't like the way it was done, but you can't argue with its effectiveness. I don't expect there will be much lawlessness around here for quite a while."

"No trial? That's bad, they should have had a trial," Revelation said. "But I'm glad it's over. I want little Matthew to grow up to be a gentlemen rancher in a civilized country."

James chuckled. "You want him to be a gentleman rancher, huh? Well, then I guess that means I'm going to have to make North Shadows a gentleman's ranch."

"Oh, it already is," Revelation said.

"What do you mean?"

"Well, it is a ranch, isn't it? And you, my darling husband, are the most gentlemanly person I've ever known. That makes it a gentleman's ranch."

Under the padded quilt, Revelation moved closer to James. All was well in the house of Cason.

SIGNET

Joseph A. West

"I look forward to many years of entertainment from Joseph West."
—Loren D. Estleman

"Western fiction will never be the same."
—Richard S. Wheeler

Silver Arrowhead
0-451-20569-3

When the bones of the world's first Tyrannosaurus Rex are discovered in Montana cattle country—and the paleontologist responsible for the find is murdered—it's up to San Francisco detective Chester Wong to find the killer.

Johnny Blue and the Hanging Judge
0-451-20328-3

In this new adventure, Blue and his sidekick find themselves on trial in the most infamous court in the West....

To order call: 1-800-788-6262